No Substitute for Milestones

No Substitute for Milestones

Carolyn J. Rose

2019

No Substitute for Milestones

www.deadlyduomysteries.com

Cover design by Dorion D. Rose, Broken Cork Photography

Interior design for print edition by Boulevard Photografica/Patty G. Henderson

Digital editions (epub and mobi) produced by Booknook.biz

Paperback edition ISBN: 978-0-9995310-7-5
Mobi edition ISBN: 978-0-9995310-8-2
Epub edition ISBN: 978-0-9995310-9-9

Many thanks to
Pam Brisby Laughlin

Chapter 1

"I get it, sir. I understand," I told the irate man on line two. "You want to participate in the swap show. You want to trade guns for knives or grenades or even land mines. You've made that clear each of the five times you went through it. There's no need to repeat it all."

But apparently he felt there was, and he started from the top. I rolled my eyes, aimed my index finger at my temple, and pulled an imaginary trigger. Through the glass panel that separated my producing booth from the talent studio, I saw Muriel Ballantine shoot me a fleeting but sympathetic smile. Since she was also a woman without an excess of patience, she knew how difficult it was for me to be polite—or at least not openly hostile—for a solid three hours. And it was especially difficult to keep my temper and sarcasm in check with people like this guy, people who didn't listen and/or wouldn't take "no" for an answer.

I turned my attention to a second window. The board op on the other side mimed hanging himself with a length of cable—cable I assumed wasn't crucial to keeping *Hot to Swap* on the air. Despite the bushy hair that often obscured his eyes and his air of nonchalant incompetence, the board op—he actually went by the name Op—was a professional. By replacing, splicing, and working around, he kept the radio station's aging equipment functioning.

His efforts kept the signal beaming from the tower for listeners in Reckless River, Washington.

My job, call screening for the Saturday morning swap show, wasn't rocket science. I greeted callers, explained the rules, asked them to limit their swapping to two items a week, logged their names, numbers, and swap items in the computer, and put them in line to go on the air with Mrs. Ballantine. Most didn't argue about what they were and weren't allowed to offer for trade. And most who did argue gave in. Or they gave up. And sometimes hung up. But this guy . . .

"We appreciate your interest in the program." I jumped into the fray once more. "But as I told you five times, this radio station, and this swap show, operate under federal rules and regulations as well as policies of our own. The bottom line is this—we don't trade weapons."

He muttered a few expletive-laden sentences about the government, the Second Amendment, and the short-sightedness of inflexible women who couldn't see their way clear to making an exception. All the while, buttons for the other three phone lines blinked—two with a pulse indicating callers were holding to chat with Mrs. B and offer items to trade, and line four with a frequency indicating it was in need of answering. Believe me, I wanted to do just that, but first I had to ditch the guy on line two, ditch him in a way that wouldn't leave him disgruntled. Or at least not so disgruntled he'd tool down here and flatten car tires. Or ask my name so he could post on social media that Barbara Reed was the rudest radio show call screener in the Pacific Northwest.

Not that I had any intention of giving this guy my name. No, if it came down to it, I'd give him my sister's name. I might even offer her phone number as well. That would fix him. Even a few seconds on the line with her would make him want to slice off his dialing finger.

"How about pills?" he asked. "Can I trade them? Because I got some pain killers left from the time I accidentally shot—"

"No pills. The regulations—"

I disconnected in the middle of the sentence.

Technically, in a splitting-hairs kind of way, I'd just hung up on myself, not on him.

Not that he'd recognize the distinction. And not that he wouldn't call back. And sound off at length. Probably also at volume.

But first he had to get through on one of the dedicated lines. And, thanks to the quirks of the radio station's phone system, I had ways of making sure that didn't happen.

I put the line I'd just cleared on hold and pounced on line four. "*Hot to Swap*. We have a few minutes left. Hopefully we'll get to your call. What do you want to trade?"

"You. For just about anything or anyone," my sister said.

I clapped my hand over my mouth to muffle a retort and, as I had many times, wondered if thinking about Iz summoned her. Did my thoughts create vibrations or even a magnetic field? Was I unwittingly putting thoughts together into some kind of an incantation?

"I don't think I could do worse than you," she went on.

I had exactly the same sentiment about her. Under the word "overbearing" in the dictionary there should be a picture of Indigo Zephyr. That's the name Jeannine Reed gave herself when she launched her checkered career as a public speaker, feminine myth interpreter, women's rights proponent, protest leader, and rabble rouser. Don't get me wrong, she'd had a positive influence on the lives of a lot of women. But on my life during the past two decades? Not so much.

"What time are you getting home?" she asked. "We need to talk."

Meaning she intended to speechify at length and expected me to hang on every word and agree with every opinion, proposal, or plan.

(For the record, I seldom met those expectations. When my parents checked out emotionally after my brother's death, Iz had stepped in to keep my ten-year-old self from starvation, neglect, and grievous harm caused by doing stupid stuff. So I owed her. I was also in her debt for saving me from a killer who tried to send me to the bottom of the Columbia River. But I figured that listening just enough to take in every tenth or twentieth word balanced the scales. And, since she specialized in belaboring points, that's about all I required to get one of hers.)

I glanced through the oblong window to the studio where Mrs. B, diamond rings flashing as she patted Cheese Puff's scruffy orange head, enthused into the microphone, doing her best to make a piece of trash resemble treasure. And her best was darn good. Since *Hot to Swap* went on the air in June, she—with adoring glances from my entitled ten-pound mutt—had helped listeners unload everything from microwaves to manicure sets, and books to bongo drums. My wealthy neighbor had no experience hosting a radio show, but she had a flair for it. And, despite the facts that she owned the place and took no monetary compensation, she worked as hard as a new employee hoping to climb the take-home-pay ladder. She had a way of making people feel that they, and the items they wanted to swap, were important, special, and even unique.

Unlike my sister.

Iz had a flair for making people feel they were like dog poop on the bottom of her shoes.

"That boyfriend of yours isn't holding up his end of our project," she grumped.

Meaning Dave Martin, the county's homicide and major crimes detective, had expectations that Iz would hold up *her* half of their efforts to round up grant money for programs aimed at cutting crimes affecting senior citizens. Iz had been in the process of reinventing herself as a home health aide when she'd come across a scam artist targeting wealthy local residents. Dave, whose concerns about rising crimes against seniors had been shuffled aside by his former supervisor, made the arrest. The stories crafted by reporter Stan Stewart for the *Reckless River Roundup* got national attention. That prompted county officials to demand more proactive policing. In the rush to jump on the bandwagon, someone suggested Iz become an advocate/investigator attached to the major crimes division of the sheriff's department.

In other words, attached to Dave.

Trust me, Dave hadn't been the one to make that suggestion. He would rather take out his own gallbladder with his teeth than spend time in the vicinity of my sister. But the sheriff had jumped on the idea like a fox on a field mouse. And Dave was in no financial position to walk away in order to get away. To date, he'd crunched numbers to demonstrate the need for the project and completed two grant applications for regional organizations. To date, my sister had talked about pursuing hefty and long-term grants from national organizations. Although I'd offered to proof and polish her drafts, I'd seen nothing on paper.

I glanced at the blinking lights on the phone console then checked the clock. Seven minutes to go.

"You owe me for sacrificing three days of my life in Missouri with Mom and Dad. Just so you could have a little dental work."

That was hardly accurate. That "little" dental work involved root canals and extractions. I'd been sore for two weeks.

"And I can't believe I thought you had a real summer job. All you did was play with kids. For nothing."

Also not accurate. Although there had been some play involved, my summer volunteer job was all about creating and supervising activities for kids, kids who might have been on the streets if my friend Ardie hadn't designed a fun and food program.

"You didn't have to visit them," I said in as firm a voice as I could manage. "I could have taken off a few days once I had things organized. I would have gone." Although not willingly. After a meal and ten minutes of catching up, a visit with my parents entered the awkward zone. And it stayed there until they dropped me at the airport.

How awkward is that zone? Well, imagine you're crossing a stage to receive a major award and you have a wardrobe malfunction of epic proportions. Now imagine you realize you misheard and the award is actually for someone else. Now imagine you fall down the stairs on your way back to your seat and sprawl across the actual recipient.

"Well, the point is, you didn't go," Iz said. "I took the bullet."

(For the record, by citing schedule conflicts, she'd dodged that particular bullet for nearly 20 years. Granted, given her conferences and demonstrations and my parents' endless rounds of golf, cards, square dancing, dinners, and amateur theater productions, schedule conflicts were thick on the ground. And, to be honest, I'm pretty sure my parents had been okay with only an occasional call or card. The text they sent me after Iz returned said they were pleased their daughters had grown into strong and independent women and it was time for all of us to follow the courses of our individual lives. I interpreted that to mean they felt we didn't need them and they didn't need us. After I got past feeling a little bit lost and hurt, I felt a comfortable sense of relief.)

"You need to talk to Dave about this," Iz went on.

"And say what?"

"Well, first remind him that I was the one who uncovered the scam artist. All he did was show up at the last minute and snap on handcuffs. I set the trap. And I took my life in my hands to do it. I could have been seriously injured."

Only because she fell across a table loaded with porcelain knickknacks and glass-encased clocks. The damage to the collectibles ran to several thousand dollars. The damage to my sister's body was minimal. But the damage to her ego was priceless. So was my memory of how her can't-fail plan ended with her flat on her back.

"I should get more respect," Iz complained in a demanding tone of voice.

Meaning she wanted continual praise and a pass on doing more than a minimal amount of work.

"Second, explain to Dave that he needs to focus on this project and forget all the other stuff. He needs to stop running around, and stop wasting time writing reports."

"By 'running around' do you mean responding to calls to investigate suspicious deaths and other crimes? And by 'writing reports' do you mean filing information on his investigations?"

Iz hesitated. For about three seconds. "I bet he could make those reports shorter. And I bet some of those crimes aren't anywhere near as important as my project."

I suppressed another retort and told myself it was pointless to explain that Dave couldn't pick and choose which crime scenes he responded to. It was also pointless to mention that the reports Dave wrote could be crucial to the prosecution of the crimes he investigated.

"Dave could work evenings and weekends," Iz said. "Instead of just hanging out."

Meaning spending time with me. Or his daughter Allison. Or unwinding from the responsibilities and stress of a job that consumed far more than 40 hours each week. Time he gave gladly in the interest of making our little piece of Southwest Washington a safer place.

"So, what time will you be home so we can have a talk?"

It seemed we—or at least Iz—just had a talk. Replaying the one-sided conversation would only exacerbate the grinding headache that sprouted and put down roots in my brain when I heard my sister's voice.

I glanced at the blinking buttons on my phone, saw one go dark as Mrs. B finished with the caller, and punched it to hold.

"Well?" Iz demanded. "It's a simple question. You get off work in five minutes. What time will you be at your condo?"

Chapter 2

Knowing Iz wouldn't believe it, I handed her the truth. "I don't know."

"You don't know? You don't have a down-to-the-minute time of arrival because you're going to lunch or shopping? Or you don't know because you're trying to come up with a time that will be inconvenient for me?"

(For the record, I wasn't. Not because that wasn't a dandy idea, but because I doubt there's a time my sister would consider "inconvenient" if the objective was to annoy me. Although she preferred to sleep late, Iz would rise well before dawn if it meant she could bother, badger, or bedevil me. And, although she had home health care clients to visit, I was confident she'd rearrange their schedules to make time to shred me like a cabbage on its way to becoming coleslaw.)

"I'm saying I don't know because I don't know. As soon as we're off the air I'm heading for the picket line at Captain Meriwether High School."

"What? Why are *you* picketing? You're not a real teacher!"

"I am so," I responded in a childish voice. "I may not have a teaching position, but I'm a certified teacher. And I'm going to walk the picket line with my friends until they get a contract offer they can live with."

"But what—"

"You're not against teachers, are you? Or against unions?" I hauled in a breath and played a card she couldn't trump without turning her core belief systems inside out. "Or have you changed your mind about the right of people to protest? And what about demonstrating solidarity with union members?"

She grunted.

I charged on before she could remind me of her long history of championing underdogs. "Anyway, that's where I'll be and I have no idea how long they'll keep up the demonstration. So if you really want to talk, come to Captain Meriwether High School and walk the line with me."

By now you should be well aware that one of the last things I wanted—right after women losing the vote, the sea level rising two feet, or a law that fennel must be included with every meal—was my sister on the picket line beside me. But I figured it was a safe offer. Much as Iz enjoyed making me sweat, she hated anything resembling work or exercise that made her do the same.

"I'm all for teachers," she retorted. "But I have better things to do this afternoon. Just remember to tell your boyfriend what I said."

"I'll remember."

At least I'd remember her demand.

But would I tell him?

The odds were against it.

Dave didn't need me piling on secondhand aggravation from my sister. He got plenty of firsthand guff.

"But make no mistake. We need to have a talk. And we will. Soon."

Iz punctuated that threat by disconnecting. I reveled in silence for half a second, then put her empty line on hold and glanced at the clock. Two and a half minutes until we were off the air. In his tiny sound-proofed cubicle, the board op was chair dancing to music I couldn't hear but suspected—given the way he was thrashing an air guitar—was something by The Who. He shot me an okay sign and mimed lifting a glass and draining it. Knowing his love of designer beer and his quest to sample every offering from every brew pub in Reckless River, I made a mental note not to get between him and the door when the hands on the clock came together at the top of the dial.

A button went dark as Mrs. B picked up the final call. Immediately it blinked, signaling an in-coming call. I glanced at my computer screen and recognized the number as belonging to the man I'd hung up on. Fortunately, time was on my side. Only two minutes remained until we were off the air.

I jabbed the button and rattled off "*Hot to Swap*. I'm sorry but we're out of time. Please call back next Saturday."

Before he could utter even a syllable, I pushed the button again, disconnecting. In the next second I put the line on hold, locking him out. Not my finest moment. But sometimes—if the goal is to avoid an argument and the fallout that might follow—dishonesty is the best policy.

I waved at Mrs. B and wiggled two fingers.

Not that she needed a time cue. She seemed to have an internal clock that never needed rewinding, but wore a diamond-studded wristwatch to back up her instincts. Still, giving her cues was part of my job description, and it paid to follow the rules—especially on a day when I'd cited them to keep a caller off the air.

To further cover my posterior on that particular issue, I shot a quick memo to Dario O'Brien and copied Deming Featherstone. As you know if you've been following the story of my life, Dario is a bear of a man who manages the radio station and makes Mrs. B a very happy woman. Deming is an eager youngster with a British accent and a bad coffee habit who produces the weekday morning talk show hosted by my ex-husband Jake Stranahan. Often, Deming makes Jake a very unhappy man. That's because Deming's job involves keeping Jake from violating federal regulations. He does that by monitoring a tape delay designed to head off inappropriate comments. He also examines, and usually shoots down, Jake's schemes aimed at promoting himself and increasing his listening audience.

As you probably also know by now, Jake's moral streak is pretty narrow. In fact, it makes the line drawn by a fine-tip pen seem like a four-lane highway. Consequently, many of his schemes also involve ways for him to line his pockets, rake in freebies, and attract women. If those women have ready cash and are willing to pony up for dinners, shows, spa treatments, car repairs, and overnight stays at Portland hotels, so much the better. Deming was a bright guy, but managing Jake was as challenging as herding sidewinders across a cactus-studded desert in the dark of the moon.

Anyway, after I explained why I hadn't allowed the caller to argue his way on the air, I warned them he might call during business hours to complain. With any luck, he'd have cooled off by then. And if he hadn't, I felt confident Dario could handle him. A teddy bear at heart, he'd cultivated a tone with an undercurrent of menace that had a way of discouraging bullies and time wasters.

The red second hand hit the four and Mrs. B thanked the last caller, provided a brief forecast for the rest of the weekend—hot and dry—and suggested everyone cool off in their basements while searching for items to swap next week.

"I can't wait to learn what you find and what someone else wants to swap for it," she said. And I knew she meant it. Mrs. B had fallen in love with the swap show and so had listeners. The program Dario had envisioned mainly as a way to focus her energy—thus avoiding a repeat of her disastrous hobby-of-the-week period—was growing an audience.

The board op potted up the theme music as she spoke, then switched the station to the satellite programming that filled most on-air hours. He bowed toward Mrs. B, gave me a nod, turned out the overhead light in his booth, and scurried away in search of a brew.

Lacking a scheduled communion with hops and yeast, I moved at a slower pace, shutting down the computer and wiping the console, phone, and keyboard with a disposable cloth from a pop-up dispenser. I wasn't in Deming's league when it came to neatness—his desk was a study in geometric angles—but I was all for trying to keep the germ population under control. And I liked to leave the place as spotless as I found it.

When I entered the studio, Mrs. B was also wiping up, paying special attention to the microphone.

"You did that when you came in," I reminded her. "After you tossed a week's worth of old scripts and food wrappers. If Jake doesn't leave the studio in decent shape for you, why do you clean up for him?"

I didn't add "I wouldn't," but I didn't have to. Mrs. B knew that after being lied to, cheated on, and bilked out of my savings, I wasn't inclined to do anything for my ex-husband. At least not anything positive. Sure, he'd paid back money siphoned from my bank account, but there was no way to pay down the pain and humiliation I'd suffered. And money paid back couldn't make up for money that wasn't there when I'd needed it the most. They say time heals all wounds, but all the years left in my life wouldn't be enough to grow scar tissue over the gouges Jake inflicted on my soul.

(For the record, and in what little defense there is for his actions, Jake seldom sets out with the intention of doing harm to others. That's mainly because Jake is all about Jake. He views others mainly as his audience and admirers. It's also because Jake isn't possessed of a mind capable of thought more complex than realizing that a PB&J classic sandwich requires bread, peanut butter, *and* jelly.)

Mrs. B didn't suggest I make more of an effort to shed the past. She lifted my entitled mutt from a pale blue puffy pillow—the one with an embroidered slogan reading "I'm in charge and don't you forget it"—and placed him on her chair. "I'm simply setting an example."

I rolled my eyes as she packed the pillow in a cabinet and wiped the area where it had been. I didn't say that Jake wouldn't notice and/or wouldn't care. Following her example would involve effort and wouldn't result in financial benefit. Plus, I was certain he'd feel cleaning was far beneath him.

Sometimes—usually as I scrubbed the bathrooms in my condo—I wondered what my life would be like if I was more like my ex. I wondered how it would feel not to be burdened by obligations and expectations, to be able to let more things slide or blithely shove them off on others.

"There." Mrs. B dropped the wipe in the trash, patted her silvery hair, and gathered up Cheese Puff, her purse, and a pair of designer sunglasses. "Shall we go to lunch? My treat."

"I'd love to." And not just because she'd pick up the tab. Time spent with Mrs. B was usually quality time—if I could steer the conversation away from the wedding date Dave and I had yet to set. "But I promised I'd walk the picket line this afternoon."

"I applaud your commitment, dear, but you must be hungry."

That was a safe assumption. I was almost always hungry. Well, not hungry in an Oliver Twist kind of way. Hungry as in puckish, craving, caught with a case of the munchies, or yearning for something crunchy and salty and, okay, covered with orange cheesy dust.

She nuzzled Cheese Puff's head. "I know I'm in need of sustenance. And the little prince is longing for a special treat."

Cheese Puff opened his mouth to display his gold-capped tooth and licked his lips. Mrs. B's idea of a special treat was generally along the lines of rare roast beef or chicken Kiev or a slice of steak imported from Japan.

I had more plebeian tastes—and a far more plebeian income. "I'll call the sandwich shop and get something to go."

"And bolt it down on the way?"

That, indeed, had been my plan. But her tone implied bolting was tantamount to throwing myself from a freeway overpass during rush hour. Mrs. B, Empress of Etiquette, would never bolt a meal, no matter how hungry. Okay, I did once see her swallow half a bottle of beer in a few gulps, but that was for medicinal purposes. She needed it to head off a nervous breakdown after driving with Allison.

"I have a better idea," she said in a no-arguments-will-be-heard tone. "I assume you have a menu for the sandwich shop in your car."

That was like saying she assumed I breathed.

I nodded.

"Good. You go to the demonstration and take lunch orders. Text me at the sandwich shop and I'll deliver."

"Okay. But there might be 20 or 30 teachers on the line."

She patted her purse. "Are you worried about my bank balance?"

I laughed. Thanks to her late husband Marco and his knack for buying low and selling high, Mrs. B's bank balance was beyond the valley of substantial. Her financial situation was way down on my list of things to be concerned about. It came right after worrying whether Pluto knew it had been demoted from planetary status. "Will you have enough room in your car for all the sandwiches and drinks?"

"If there isn't, I'll hire a taxi."

And she would.

"Okay. Be sure you don't park on school property."

"Got it. I assume you want tuna on rye like usual."

I opened my mouth to say I wasn't as predictable as she made out, but tuna had been on my mind. Still, just to prove I wasn't in a rut, I said, "Not rye. Sourdough. With tomato and cucumber. And I want barbecue chips, not plain ones."

"Got it." Her lips lifted in a maddening smile. "Now run along and do your part to help the teachers."

Chapter 3

I obeyed her order and ran along. Or, rather, I prepared to drive along, nibbling on a few emergency cheese crackers from a container in the glove compartment and checking my e-mail and the school district website before I started my car.

School was supposed to start on Wednesday, but no one knew if it would. Negotiations had gone on late into the night and picked up again this morning. The board had been slated to meet at noon and should right now be considering the latest offer from the union. Although some of my teacher friends assured me a compromise was close, the wording of the official updates was so cautious I couldn't distinguish lines to read between. So I didn't know if their assumption was on the money.

When I reached Captain Meriwether High School, I spotted about two dozen teachers walking along the public sidewalk and waving signs at passing vehicles. The signs bore slogans like SUPPORT YOUR TEACHERS and IF YOU CAN READ THIS, STAND UP FOR TEACHERS. Most drivers stayed in their lanes and honked their horns in support but, as I joined the line, one jabbed his middle finger in the air and swung close. His tires scraped the curb before he wrenched the wheel and veered away in a cloud of noxious exhaust.

Aston Marsden raised his arm to respond with a single digit of his own, but Gertrude Suttle hip checked him. Like me, Gertrude carries a few extra pounds below the waist, so the bump was enough to unbalance the history teacher and make him spin aside. Yelping all the while, he executed a shuffle step to keep his balance. "Why'd you do that?"

"Because of what you were about to do. This is a peaceful demonstration. We ignore people like that. We don't engage." She made a chopping motion with her sign. "If you'd gotten here at 10:45 when you were supposed to, you'd know the rules."

"I had things to do this morning. Important things."

Gertrude's expression was as skeptical as her tone. "Well, when you got here after doing all those important things, you should have asked if there were any important things you should know before you picked up a sign."

Aston muttered under his breath, complaining about too many people making too many rules and too many other people acting like imbeciles and nobody doing anything about it.

Gertrude sighed. "I know it's tough for you, Aston. It's tough for all of us. But we agreed the best approach is to remain calm and in control when we're confronted by jerks."

"You mean I'm supposed to go all Gandhi and turn the other cheek and stuff?"

"Exactly."

Aston curled his lips in an expression of disgust similar to one I'd adopt if the only choices for dinner were liver, lima beans, or liver stuffed with lima beans.

"If you can't manage to do that," Gertrude lectured, "you might as well go home and sit out the strike."

"Can't sit." He rubbed his left hip, scowled, and raised his sign once more, the fringe on his buckskin jacket fluttering. "Might as well walk."

Although I wondered why Aston said he couldn't sit, I didn't wonder why he was wearing a jacket on a sunny day when the temperature was expected to hit a mark somewhere above 90. His wardrobe selection had nothing to do with common sense and everything to do with his avocation. Whenever he could, he joined others with an interest in reenacting bits of history, especially anything to do with Civil War battles, pathfinders, fur trappers, prospectors, and mountain men in general. Aston contended that wearing buckskin and eating hardtack, jerky, roots, and greens plucked from the roadside helped him stay in character.

Not that he turned down conventional food. At lunchtime in the teachers' room I'd seen him devour stray chips, sandwich crusts, and random strands of pasta from the bottom of a bowl. The only foods he didn't touch—along with the rest of us—were those offered by Brenda Waring.

(If that name rings a bell, you already know why we steer clear of her culinary offerings. If you haven't been clued in earlier, I'll bring you up to speed soon.)

I waved my phone and a copy of the Reckless River Sandwich Shop menu and shouted that Mrs. B planned a picnic for everyone and I was taking orders. Aston elbowed the horticulture teacher aside. "Roast beef. Rare. On rye. With cheddar. None of that Swiss stuff. And mustard. Hot mustard. No mayo."

"Because mountain men didn't have mayonnaise in the wilderness?" I baited him as I texted his order.

"Because it's sissy stuff." He ruffled his scruffy beard with his fingers, releasing a shower of bark bits, moss, and bread crumbs from this morning's breakfast or perhaps last night's dinner. "Got no kick."

Being a big fan of quality mayonnaise, I thought he was wrong about the lack of a kick. But starting an argument with Aston was like starting into the Amazon jungle without a compass, a machete, a single ounce of water, or an iota of common sense. "What do you want with your sandwich? Chips? Cola? Cookies?"

"Sure. All that." He scratched an oozing red eruption on his neck. "Bee sting." He pushed up his left sleeve to show me a larger swelling just above his wrist. It was the color of a plum past its prime and marred by two darker spots. "Snake."

"Thanks for sharing," Ardette Johnson said. "Now step aside and let the rest of us order before you drop your pants and we lose our appetites into the middle of next year."

Limping, Aston grumped off down the sidewalk. Ardie ordered egg salad on whole wheat and lemonade while Gertrude filled me in. "He hit the mountain man's version of a trifecta last week. He got stung by bees, bitten by a snake, and had his butt gashed by an osprey."

"An osprey?"

"Right." Gertrude flapped her arms. "An osprey. A big bird."

"I know what an osprey is. I see them swooping down for fish in the river. Why was Aston attacked? Did he get too close to a nest?"

"No. He was in the water." Ardie handed me her sign and snatched my phone, her glittery deep purple nail polish sparkling in the sunlight. "I'll do this. I'm faster."

I didn't argue. She was right. Ardie in motion—and except when she slept she was always in motion—was a streak of black lightning. I met her when I subbed at the juvenile jail, but for nearly a year now she'd worked as a classroom aide at Captain Meriwether. She went above and beyond every day.

"Get back in the line with Doug and he'll fill you in. He was there when the osprey struck."

So, while Ardie tapped in Gertrude's order, I hoisted her sign and caught up with English teacher Doug Whitman who was marching behind Brenda Waring. "Ardie says you witnessed the aerial attack on Aston."

"I did. Yesterday. A day that will live in infamy." Doug grinned and settled his sign on his shoulder. "Remember how Aston and I took some kids from the summer rec project to that sandy beach up near the wildlife refuge?"

"Yes. You left after I took my group to the library to return their books. You were still gone when I finished straightening up the room and went home."

"Right."

Doug executed a sudden quarter turn and sidestepped along the walk, moving his sign to screen him from the oncoming traffic. A girl in a coppery pink car smiled and waved as she passed, her hand moving fast enough to shake a cocktail. She appeared vaguely familiar. Perhaps I'd subbed in one of her classes.

I waved back.

She shook her head, lowered her hand, crimped her lips, and accelerated away.

"Was that a friend of yours?" I asked Doug.

"No." He rested his sign on his shoulder again and continued his story. "Things went sideways almost from the start. I had a program worked up on rocks and minerals and Aston had a couple of gold pans so the kids could try their luck panning for color. But he got off on a tangent."

"Naturally," Brenda Waring snarked over her shoulder. "Without tangents he'd have no conversation at all. No life at all."

Doug and I exchanged eye rolls, acknowledging that the relationship switch between Aston and Brenda was in the "off" position. If nourishment was the only factor, a match between a man who could survive on what he scavenged in the wild and a health and cooking instructor who specialized in weird foods and even weirder food combinations would seem like a natural fit. But their personalities cancelled out points of attraction.

"The man is stuck in the past." Brenda adjusted a red tank top a size too small for her curves and tugged at the cuffs of a pair of shorts the color of lemons. Ardie, who stuck to basic black with an occasional foray into mulberry or magenta, once described Brenda's style as "flamboyantly form-fitting."

"Give Ardie your order," Doug told her, "so we get lunch delivered before the sun goes down."

Brenda veered from the line, muttering something about the choices at the sandwich shop being bland and completely lacking in cutting-edge culinary creativity.

Doug performed more eyeball acrobatics. "Wasn't it creativity that landed her in the hospital in June when she made those tarts to spice up the senior breakfast?"

"Yes, but she insists the emergency room doctor overreacted. According to her, it wasn't food poisoning, just a simple stomach upset from a combination of ingredients." I mimed gagging myself. "And if it means I can avoid further discussion, I'm willing to go along with that. After all, I got paid for a full day of subbing while she was at the hospital. And none of the seniors so much as nibbled at the tarts, so she was the only one affected."

I tapped my sign against his. "Now, tell me the rest of the story."

"Okay, so Aston started telling the kids about D.B. Cooper and how a kid uncovered money from the hijacking along the river back in 1980. A few of the kids started digging but they got bored and started splashing each other and one got caught in a current. Aston kicked off his boots and went in after him. Got to the kid in no time. The man's a strong swimmer."

I didn't doubt that. Aston didn't have bulky muscles, but he was wiry and he probably tested his mountain man skills by swimming across lakes and fording streams in flood season. "Where does the osprey come in?"

"Right after he got the kid to shallow water so I could drag him up on the beach," Doug said with a grin. "See, Aston was wearing a pair of authentic deerskin pants he sewed himself. No zipper. No elastic. Not even a button. Only a drawstring. And it came untied."

He paused, snickering and shaking his head, testing what little patience I had.

"So, his pants came off?"

"Not all the way off. Just down around his ankles."

"That's close enough to 'off' for me. I get the picture."

"No." His grin broadened. "I don't think you get the whole picture."

Chapter 4

Doug paused, his grin widening.

It was tough. I used up two days' worth of willpower keeping my lips zipped. But I didn't beg. I didn't even whimper and make with sad eyes.

Doug caved. "Aston went commando yesterday."

Arrggghhh.

I closed my eyes and rubbed them. It made no difference. The image of Aston's hind end had already seared itself into my brain. It burned with such intensity, and burned so far down, I estimated I'd need an uninterrupted hour of gazing at images of Chris Hemsworth as Thor to make it fade even a little. I longed to race home and gaze while drinking a frothy beverage. But first I had to know more. "Where does the osprey come in?"

Doug's snicker morphed into a chuckling snort and he clapped a hand over his mouth and held his breath until his eyes bulged. "So," he finally said with a wheeze, "Aston's in about three feet of water, just enough to cover stuff no kid needs to see and no supervising adult wants them to see. Unless the goal is to get arrested. Know what I mean?"

"I do."

"Anyway, he bends way over to grab his pants and—" Doug snickered and slapped his hand on his mouth again, this time for only a few seconds. Then he finished in a rush. "Aston's backside is white. Scary white. Like the belly of a fish. And ospreys eat . . .?"

He pointed at me, waiting with the kind of expectant gaze he'd turn on a distracted student in the back row.

"Fish," I said.

"Correct."

"You think the bird mistook Aston's butt for a fish?"

"Correct again. A bloated and hairy fish."

"Enough."

I rubbed my eyes once more knowing that now the image would remain clear and sharp. Unless I had radical brain surgery, I was stuck with it for life. And, given the mysterious way my mind worked, I couldn't predict when it would pop up to ruin an experience. I might be about to taste the first long-anticipated morsel from a bag of new and improved cheesy snacks. I might be in bed with Dave about to—

"Bird probably thought he—or she—could dine on that fish for days." Apparently unaffected by gag-producing mental imagery, Doug went on as if he was talking about something as mundane as sharpening a pencil. "As it is, Aston won't be sitting down for a week or more."

He hauled in a breath and straightened. "I shouldn't laugh. He was in a lot of pain. Had to have 20 stitches and he's got enough antibiotic pills and salve to start his own pharmacy. Who knows what that bird had his talons into before Aston?"

While I was trying not to think about that, Ardie tapped my shoulder. "Finished. Unless you want to include him." She pointed to the man slouching our way across the street. It was reporter Stan Stewart, wearing his signature baggy corduroy slacks and a jacket—today greenish tweed—with sagging pockets and permanent wrinkles around the elbows. "If I take his order, will he take our side in his article?"

I shook my head. Stewart—he preferred to go by his last name—made every effort to be impartial. At least in his articles in the *Reckless River Roundup*. Off the record I suspect he leaned toward the underdog. And, in my view, since teachers hadn't had a significant raise in many years, they had underdog status. "No, he'll present both sides. So a bribe would be wasted, but Mrs. B is buying lunch and she—"

"Wouldn't approve of letting anyone go hungry," Ardie finished. "I'll make it clear this is on her dime, not ours."

"Because we can't afford it," Doug hoisted his sign. "Unless we get a raise."

"A raise that doesn't all go to taxes and cost-of-living increases," Gertrude added. Then her tart voice softened. "At least I have a job. And some semblance of health insurance. And a pension. But don't get me started."

I smiled and gave her a one-armed hug. Gertrude managed the Family Support Room, taking in donations and handing them out to students and families struggling to bring financial ends somewhere close to meeting. For all my money woes, I had never found myself on the street and never missed a meal. Although, to be honest, some of my meals had lacked variety and been less than nutritious or tasty.

"After I wrap up the lunch order, I'm heading for a pit stop at the service station down the way," Ardie said. "You can keep my sign while I'm away. Remember to stay off the grass. It may be brown and as good as dead, but every blade belongs to the school district."

I nodded, raised her sign, and trudged on. Ardie intercepted Stewart at the edge of the sidewalk and took what appeared to be a substantial order. I wasn't surprised. His hunger for free food was right up there with his hunger for a good story. That's why I also wasn't surprised when he sidled over to the picket line, got in step beside me, handed over my phone, raised one eyebrow, and asked, "So . . . ?"

I knew what he was after, but played the clueless card. "So . . . what?"

He glanced around as if ours was a top-secret conversation of great interest to other reporters. I wondered if he expected to spot a black van with a camera lens sticking out of one window, or maybe a high-tech recording device aimed our way from a power pole. "So, what are you working on?"

I answered with all the naïve innocence I could muster. "Right now I'm working on supporting teachers in the contract negotiations. Later I'll be working on doing a few loads of laundry, cleaning up the kitchen, maybe making something for din—"

"You know what I meant!" He made a chopping motion with his hand. "Big stuff. What big stuff are you on?"

I went on with my act. "Well, Mrs. B and Dario and Deming and I are working on plans to continue the swap show at least to the end of the year instead of killing it at the end of September. I'm not wild about working Saturdays, but the extra money is nice. And the show is going so well Deming thinks we could use it as a springboard for other local programs. Maybe a gardening-tips show or—"

"Stop playing dumb. What are you investigating? If you've stumbled across a crime, I want to know before you accidentally solve it and the cops give everyone the story. You owe me."

I didn't pay a whole lot of attention in biology class, so I don't know if humans have hackles, but if they do, you can bet those remarks raised mine. "In the first place, I do not 'stumble' across crimes. And I don't accidentally solve cases. I hear things, I notice things, and people tell me things that may be connected to criminal activity. Then I investigate in a thoughtful and logical manner."

Stewart opened his mouth, perhaps to laugh or to question the truth of my statements, but I charged on. "In the second place, you got national recognition from the stories you wrote on the senior scam. And you got a big raise. So maybe you're the one who owes me."

Stewart narrowed his eyes, but I charged on once again. "And, speaking of that story, didn't you get promoted? And didn't your editor promise you wouldn't have to cover boards and meetings? Didn't you get the crime beat and free rein to investigate crimes of all kinds?"

His eyelids drew so close together I doubted he could see more than the tip of my nose.

"So, given all that," I finished up with the tone reserved for kids found wandering the hallways when they should have been in class, "what are you doing here?"

Stewart flashed me a smug smile. "Wouldn't you like to know?"

Actually, I would. But revealing that would be a sign of weakness.

So, by supreme strength of will, I managed what I hoped was a casual shrug. Meanwhile, curiosity sparked my imagination and out-there possibilities flashed through my mind—the superintendent charged with embezzlement, a school board member or a teacher caught in a scandal, kickbacks and shoddy workmanship discovered in connection with repairs underway on the roof of the music room.

I shrugged again and followed up with a yawn. "I have other things on my mind. And I don't have time for guessing games. I have a picket line to walk."

I hoisted Ardie's sign—I'LL WALK ALL DAY FOR BETTER PAY.

"I'm not working on anything big," Stewart said in a sulking tone. "I, uh, just thought I'd come by. It's been weeks since we had a friendly chat."

I started marching, doing my best to ignore a woman in a luxury car inching along beside picketers. Her top-of-her-lungs message boiled down to a theory that public education was the biggest waste of money since the last redecorating splurge at the White House. I had to agree about the splurge, but if she got out of her car, I was ready to argue that she was making an apples-to-oranges comparison.

"To the best of my knowledge," I told Stewart, "we've talked often about crimes of various magnitudes, but we've never had what I consider a friendly chat."

"You want friendly?" He beamed a wide fake smile for half a second. It was the kind of smile that belonged on a jack-o'-lantern. "You want me to emote while I'm talking?"

"Not if that's your idea of emoting. A friendly chat might involve a sharing of hobbies or recipes or opinions about sports or fashion. You're always all about story leads, news tips, and hot gossip."

Stewart kept pace. "Okay. I get it. And I admit sometimes I tend to focus too much on my job."

I snorted. "Sometimes?"

"Okay. All the time. And before you call me on it, I guess you could say I obsess more than I focus."

"You guess?"

"Okay. I completely realize I obsess. I'm aware it's a fault. I'm working on becoming a more well-rounded person. I'm working on cultivating two-way relationships."

I did a 180, following the picket line walkers back the way we'd come. Like the others, I walked faster through patches of sunlight and lingered in the cool shade beneath trees. And, like the others, I occasionally fanned myself with my sign. Summer's end in the Pacific Northwest could be brutal. Rain hadn't been in the forecast for weeks and wasn't likely to appear until half of September had passed. "So, that's the reason you're here now? To expand your relationship horizons?"

"Exactly."

As he spoke, he checked his watch and the fingers of his right hand traced the outlines of a pen and reporter's notebook in the pocket of his jacket. I turned my head to hide a smile. Maybe someday I'd tip him about his tells and let him know how he gave himself away. But not today. “A two-way relationship generally entails openness and honesty. You know that don’t you?”

“Definitely.”

“So, why don’t you say you’re in a news drought? Why don’t you come out and admit you’re looking for a rainmaker?”

Chapter 5

Stewart didn't often recognize subtlety or social cues, but he recognized the truth. And he had the grace not to argue. "Okay. That's why I'm here. You've always come up with something. You never let me down before."

"Well, prepare for a letdown of major proportions. I don't have even a germ of an idea about anything related to crime of any kind, on any level. And by that I mean right down to petty crime like pilfering a few nuts or raisins from the bins at the grocery store."

(For the record, I don't consider sampling a single nut to check for staleness to be pilfering. You won't catch me grazing my way down the aisle scooping a little of this and a little of that. I can't help it, however, if more than a single nut emerges from the spout because of a design flaw or lever malfunction on those dispensing canisters.)

"Really?" Stewart's tone was both suspicious and wheedling.

"Really. I've got nothing. Unless you want to do a story on some of these drivers harassing the picket line."

Stewart's eyes glimmered with interest, but the glimmer faded in a second. "How about Dave? Is he working any interesting cases?"

Truthfully, I had no idea. Lately Dave's lips had been zipped tight when it came to sharing information about major crimes in the county. Plus, he'd gotten wise to most of my techniques for prying information from him while he was having a second beer, falling asleep, or engaged in bedroom activities. But no way would I let Stewart know my wiles weren't working. "If he's cracking something or wants to appeal to the public, he'd go through official channels and get the word out through the communications officer."

Stewart groaned. "It takes days for that guy to get it together. It's old news by then. And everyone gets it at the same time. Even Portland reporters who can't find Reckless River on a map. Even media leeches that set up self-serving websites and claim they're news services."

"I feel your pain."

And I did. Stewart worked hard to develop sources, ferret out stories, do in-depth research, and cover all the angles. It hurt to see hard work canceled out by a media release delivered to competitors.

"I'd be angry too. But even if everyone gets the same basic facts, you're the one with the contacts and background knowledge to flesh the story out so it's front-page stuff. Or give it legs and develop a series."

His chest inflated and he raised his chin. But only for a few seconds. "If Dave's working on something big, he'd tell you, right?"

I hesitated.

"And if he didn't tell you, you'd find out." He poked my arm with his elbow. "And you'd get involved somehow. I know you. You can't help yourself."

That last part was on the money. I couldn't help myself. Mostly I didn't even try.

Dave knew I had more curiosity than a dozen cats. He regularly brought up his concerns about me going off on

USUIE missions—Unofficial and Sometimes Uninvited Investigative Endeavors. I didn't mind the lectures about being careful and not jumping to conclusions and trying to rush justice, but I did mind his tight-lipped attitude toward sharing details of his cases. He claimed he was toeing the confidentiality line because of the sheriff's concerns, but I suspected he believed keeping me in the dark would keep me below the radar of criminals intent on covering up their crimes.

And, honestly, I understood his thought process and didn't blame him. At least not much. After all, two killers had tried to drown me in the Columbia River, and another had come within seconds of shooting me. And then there was the drug dealer—

"Hey!"

I spotted Ardie on the opposite side of the street, waving her arms and running our way at a pace I couldn't have managed on a cold day with a strong tailwind pushing me down a steep slope. Once again, I vowed to exercise more and get in better shape.

"Hey," she called again when she reached the crosswalk. "You're not going to believe this."

Westbound traffic came to a stop and Ardie, prone to believe the best of others—including those driving east at that moment—started across.

"Look out!"

Doug and Aston shouted and flung their signs into the street to get the attention of the luxury-car woman who was coming around for another verbal assault on public education. Since she was leaning toward the open passenger window, she was slow hitting her brakes. With a squeal of rubber, she skidded to a stop just over the line into the crosswalk.

Doug yelped.

Aston shouted something I won't repeat.

To her credit, Ardie didn't flinch.

Neither did she scowl at the woman.

She did, however, take her sweet time crossing to the curb. Following her example, Doug and Aston didn't hustle to collect their signs. I doubted their actions won the heart or mind of the woman. I also doubted the driver would pay more attention next time she approached a crosswalk where on-coming cars had stopped. Some drivers would never admit it, but they believed pedestrians had no business anywhere on the asphalt.

"Gather round," Ardie called. "I have the latest on the contract negotiations."

Careful to stay on the public sidewalk and not inch over onto school district property, we crowded close. Stan Stewart, pushing forward beside me, dug his pen and notebook from his pocket.

"I got the info from Big Chill," Ardie said. "She happened to be at the service station filling her tank."

"Happened my foot," Gertrude said. "I bet she was watching from her office and zipped over when she saw you."

Several others nodded or voiced agreement. Wilhelmina Frost, known as Big Chill to those who loved and feared her, was the head secretary at Captain Meriwether High School. She had her finger on the pulse of district policy and intrigue, and she often had her ear against the door of Principal Tremaine Scott's office. But even though she knew where all the bodies were buried, and even though she was close to bulletproof, she wouldn't hobnob with teachers threatening to strike when classes started. Unless hobnobbing could appear to be a chance encounter.

"I won't bet against you," Doug said. "She can't appear to take sides, but I believe the Chillster is all for us." He shot a glance at Aston who was rubbing the seat of grubby jeans at the peril of tearing stitches or infecting wounds. "At least most of us."

"Get to the point." Aston pointed to a car snugging up to the curb on a side street across the way—Mrs. B's car. Cheese Puff, front feet on the dash, seemed to be supervising the operation. "Lunch has arrived."

"Yeah. Get to the point." Stewart clicked his pen and tapped it on his notebook. "I'm on deadline."

Ardie and I exchanged an eye roll. Stewart always claimed to be on deadline. Occasionally the claim was true. I had no idea what time his deadline would be on a Saturday. And, since he said he'd come to see me in search of a story, I doubted he legitimately had one. But I was willing to bet the contents of my wallet—10 dollars, 37 cents, two safety pins, and a bent paperclip—the time until deadline could be measured in hours rather than minutes.

Ardie made him sweat for a few more seconds before she unloaded. "Okay, according to Big Chill, the school board has put off considering the latest offer."

She paused once more, paused until we chorused, "Why?"

"Because one of the board members is missing."

"Missing?" Stewart stabbed his pad with his pen. "Not absent, but missing?"

"Missing," Ardie repeated.

"What does that mean?"

"Nowhere to be found."

"So, not at the board meeting?" Aston asked before Stewart could say more.

"Seriously?" Doug smacked the side of the history teacher's head. "You don't get that if someone is missing, that person is—"

Aston smacked Doug in return. "I get it."

"Yeah. Now you do."

Gertrude shoved her way between them. "Enough. You're missing the most important question. Which board member is missing?"

Once again, Ardie made us wait. Then she crowed, "Marybeth Potter."

"You're kidding," Doug said.

Ardie shook her head. "Wasn't at the meeting her usual five minutes ahead of time, isn't at home, doesn't answer her cell." She lowered her voice and aimed her next comments at Stewart. "You didn't hear this from me, but they've notified the police. And, because the school district laps into the county, the sheriff's department is involved too."

"If she's not just running late with a dead cell battery, this could look bad for us," Gertrude said.

Not that it was an excuse, but I'd had a lot going on in my life and hadn't kept up with school district issues as I probably should have. So, at the risk of appearing as out-to-lunch as Aston just had, I asked, "Why? Why would it look bad for us?"

"She's the most conservative board member," Ardie informed me in a series of capsule statements. "Divorced. Real estate agent. Styles herself a self-made success.

Rolling in dough. Lays out a fortune on a new car every year. Wears custom-made power suits. Sprays on enough expensive perfume to qualify as a source of indoor air pollution. Always votes against spending."

"Always votes for cuts," Brenda said. "Thinks the tough don't get going *unless* the going gets tough. Really tough."

"Woman ought to be staked out on an anthill," Aston contributed.

"She makes that haranguing harpy in the car seem like rational thought personified." Doug turned to Stewart. "And, for the record, my comment was off the record."

"So was mine," Aston said. "Tossing her in a pit full of rattlers would do the job quicker than an anthill anyway."

Stewart nodded and began tapping his phone.

"She'd *cut* our salaries if she could." Ardie chopped air with the edge of her hand. "She voted to reject every offer from the union so far. Didn't appear to give any of them more than two minutes worth of consideration."

"And she would have rejected the next one too." Stewart glanced up from his phone. "When our education reporter called her early this morning she said she intended to vote against the latest union presentation, no matter what it was."

"That's not . . ." I paused before I used the word "fair" because, after all, I was old enough to know that life isn't fair—at least by my definition. I was also old enough to know some people locked themselves into positions and wouldn't budge. "But she has just one vote, right?"

"Right," Doug confirmed. "But she's the chair of the board. Small, but a bully. I think a couple of the others are scared of her."

"Let's hope she just lost track of time or had a flat tire." Gertrude crossed her fingers. "Because if anything happens to her, we'll all be suspects."

The word "suspects" brought a wolfish smile to Stewart's lips and he raised his right hand to give me a high five. "I knew you'd come through with something for me. You're a lightning rod for hard news. You're a magnet for murder."

Chapter 6

I gripped my sign with both hands. "Murder?" I squawked.

"Okay, not *always* for murder. Sometimes you're a magnet for lesser crimes like theft and assault," he amended. "Or, maybe in this case, kidnapping."

"Kidnapping?" Doug echoed. "You think Marybeth Potter has been kidnapped?"

"Anything's possible," Stewart responded in a tone that made it clear he'd love to sink his teeth in a story like that.

"Wait a minute," I said. "Are you thinking a teacher in this district would kidnap a board member in order to get a pay hike?"

"Thinking that way is my job." He raised both hands in protest. "I'm on the crime beat, not the cute-features-about-puppies beat."

"Well, you're taking your thinking to extremes. You're catapulting toward conclusions without pausing to consider other possibilities."

"I'm considering all the possibilities," he argued. "It's called preparation."

"It's more like rampant speculation." I sliced and diced air with my sign. "If you insinuate we'd resort to criminal activities in order to get a raise I'll—"

"Hey." He wrestled the sign from me. "I always present both sides of the story. I'm fair and impartial. You know that."

"I know you may think you're not biased." I wrestled the sign back. "But your word choice sometimes slants your stories and—"

"Can't have a good fight on an empty stomach." Doug pushed between us and pointed to the shady yard on the side street across the way. "Take a break. Mrs. B is setting up a feast."

To my utter lack of surprise, I saw she'd acquired several folding chairs, a table, and a paper tablecloth. She'd also borrowed Luke Dylan from his job at the sandwich shop and pressed him into service. Under her direction, he was unpacking the sandwich shop's minivan and laying out plates, napkins, and wrapped sandwiches.

Mrs. B, in case you're just joining the story of my life, put up the dough to buy out a shoddily run burger joint and convert it to a clean and classy sandwich shop managed by Luke's mother Lana. I'd met Luke at Captain Meriwether High School and again while subbing at the juvenile jail where he was awaiting trial on a trumped up charge of catnapping. After my investigation revealed he'd been framed, it took 20 long minutes of terror and the sacrifice of a pair of my favorite shoes to see justice done. Since then, Lana and Luke had been part of what I like to think of as an extended family of non-related characters.

But back to the story.

"Shall we keep the picket line going and eat in shifts?" Gertrude asked.

"Works for me." Aston dropped his sign and headed across the street. "As long as I get the first lunch shift."

"Way to demonstrate that you're part of a team," Doug said.

"His idea of teamwork is jumping on a horse and 'allowing' it to carry him," Brenda snarked. "He claims he never has to use spurs or a quirt because he and the horse become as one."

"Probably because he smells like a stable," Ardie said.

"A stable in need of cleaning," Doug added.

"Okay. Stop before I lose my appetite." Gertrude waved her arms to get everyone's attention. "Let's all take a break. Twenty minutes."

With a clatter of falling signs and a patter of running feet, teachers headed for Mrs. B's impromptu picnic. Stewart, talking on his phone, followed in their wake. Knowing my tuna sandwich would be there when I arrived, I brought up the rear with Gertrude and Ardie, mopping my forehead with the sleeve of my pale green T-shirt. Combining exercise with sunlight and scorching asphalt made me sweat. Not perspire, or glow, or glisten. This was sweat. Lots of it.

Assuming my deodorant could use a little help, I grasped the hem of the T-shirt and pulled it out and up a few inches, encouraging air toward my armpits. In a moment, I did the same with the neckline. "If Marybeth Potter has such strong negative feelings about teachers' pay—?"

"Why did she run for a seat on the board?" Gertrude finished my question. "Exactly for that reason. She promised voters she'd use her experience in business to trim the fat."

"And she sees fat everywhere," Ardie added. "I mean everywhere. Every program, every salary, every piece of equipment. She'd like to see expenditures chopped by 10% or more."

"She's living in the last century. Or maybe the one before." Gertrude stomped on the lines of the crosswalk as if they were spiders. "You'd think someone who sells real estate would know the costs of housing and utilities are going up, not down."

"The cost of everything is going up," I agreed, reminding myself once again to be thankful that Mrs. B had plenty of dough and considered me her honorary daughter. She regularly picked up the tab for dinner out, and splurged on clothing and accessories for me and for Allison. Well, mostly for Allison. My go-to wardrobe was pretty much jeans (in assorted colors), T-shirts (also in assorted colors) and shirts to wear over T-shirts (in—you guessed it—assorted colors, some of them even sporting stripes or checks). With the exception of a few shirts and khaki slacks he wore to work, Dave's wardrobe was about the same. Although Mrs. B often lobbied for us to fancify and diversify, we've mostly managed to resist her efforts. "Well, almost everything is getting more expensive. I got a great deal on a toaster oven last week. And TV prices in the newspaper ads this morning are amazing."

"There are bargains if you hunt," Gertrude agreed. "But overall, costs are rising. So even if we get the raise we want—"

"Which we won't," Ardie said.

"It will be eaten up by increases in property taxes and insurance and food and gasoline."

"But don't get her started." Ardie seized her friend's arm. "Let's get our sandwiches before Aston decides anything still on the table is in the public domain."

Mrs. B would never let that happen, but from the scowls I saw through dusty windshields, I knew we'd held up traffic long enough, so I said nothing and hustled along with them. When we reached the table, we found each sandwich wrapper labeled with a teacher's name, and plenty of extra bags of chips and cans of soda.

"Pull up a lawn." Mrs. B pointed to the shady yard she'd parked in front of. Several teachers had already staked claims on the chairs she'd brought and on two wooden benches beneath a grape arbor. Others lounged against the trunks of three huge maples. "I had a lovely chat with the owner and she's delighted to offer support."

I wasn't surprised. Mrs. B had a way of charming strangers and making most of them into friends in a manner of minutes. Next week they might be lunching or shopping together.

"Feel free to sit on the porch if you like. And do come in to wash up," a pink-cheeked woman called from beside the open front door. "Make yourselves at home."

Cheese Puff, I noted, had already done that. He reclined in the woman's arms, resting against her ample bosom, eyes half closed with pleasure as she scratched his ears.

"My granddaughter teaches fourth grade over in Montana. I know how hard she works, and I'm behind you all the way. So don't be shy. Make yourselves comfortable."

"Thanks. I'll take you up on your offer to wash up," Gertrude called.

"So will I," Brenda said. "It's a long hike to the service station."

"Not long enough to peel some of that lard off your thighs." Aston mumbled through a mouthful of roast beef as he headed for a reclining lawn chair.

Brenda drew in a breath, but Gertrude tugged at her arm before she could speak. "You'll have plenty of time to trade insults when you're back on the picket line after lunch."

"And hopefully I won't hear them," Ardie muttered.

"I know what you mean." I found the sandwich marked with my name and a smiley face. "Their act is getting stale."

"Stale?" Ardie popped open a can of lemonade. "It's beyond stale. It's on life support."

"No, it's beyond that," Doug amended as we walked to a dense patch of shade at one side of the yard. "It's dead by every definition. But they haven't pulled the plug." He sat, peeled the wrapping from an egg salad sandwich, and paused with it inches from his lips. "Is it too late to ask Big Chill to assign them to another teachers' room?"

"Who else would have them?" I sat beside him and unwrapped a corner of my sandwich. Perfect. Thick slices of sourdough. Tuna salad spread in an even layer all the way to the edges. Fresh lettuce. Thinly sliced tomato and cucumber. It was a work of art.

"Maybe there's a storage room they could share." Doug took an enormous bite.

"In another building," I added.

"Keep dreaming, kids," Ardie advised as she settled. "They've got seniority over the rest of us, and neither one is hesitant about complaining—and going over Wilhelmina's head to do it."

Doug groaned and swallowed. "And Tremaine Scott's already had it up to his eyebrows with them. He's liable to blame the rest of us for their complaints and put *us* in a storage closet."

"There's a big one next to the choir room," Ardie said. "Of course, it probably still stinks of moldy choir robes."

"Not that Aston would notice over his own gamy aroma," Doug said. "But I thought they moved everything out after the leak in March."

"They did. But they moved it all back after the emergency patch job. The job that missed a spot. The robes got wet again, and no one noticed until the week before the June concert."

I'd been involved in one of my USUIEs and hadn't made it to the concert, but I'd heard others speculating about why choir members wore T-shirts and jeans. Trust Ardie to have the scoop.

And, speaking of scoops . . . "Where's Stan Stewart?"

"He's in my car, dear," Mrs. B said as she passed by offering selections from a cardboard box filled with small bags of chips. "He wanted a little privacy."

I peered over my shoulder at the car and saw the windows were up. A faint shimmering cloud escaped from the exhaust pipe. "Looks like he wanted some air conditioning, too."

"It *is* a warm day." Mrs. B, who exhibited not a trace of perspiration on her forehead, fanned herself with a napkin. "And his face was quite flushed."

"Wouldn't be overheated if he ditched that jacket," Doug said.

"And got a pair of lightweight slacks in a color that might deflect some of the heat," Ardie added.

Doug and I exchanged glances and raised eyebrows, but neither of us mentioned that the main color in her year-round wardrobe was black. Despite that, her brow was free of moisture. And not even a trace of damp marred her crisp black cotton blouse.

I mopped my forehead once more and wondered why, with my relatively pale skin, white jeans, and pastel shirt, I seemed to absorb more heat than she did. Maybe it wasn't only about absorption. Maybe she had some way of using or distributing or releasing heat before her body's thermostat hit a mark that, in my case, signaled the need to cool down by generating enough sweat to swamp a canoe.

(For the record, I'm aware that last bit is an exaggeration. I'm also well aware that I have a tendency to exaggerate frequently. In my defense . . . Well, you and I both know I don't have a defense. So let's get on with the story.)

Doug nodded toward the car. "Wonder what he's finding out. Think he'll tell us?"

"Not if it's something the others don't have," I told him. "He's paranoid about competition."

"What competition? He works for the only newspaper in town."

True. Reckless River was the modern version of a one-horse town. Okay, maybe a two- or three-horse town. But Portland was right across the Columbia River, and it was swarming with reporters. I aimed a finger over my shoulder, pointing south. "If she stays missing more than a few hours, you'll see a herd of live trucks charging across that bridge like stampeding cattle."

Doug groaned. "And every story about her disappearance will end with speculation that it could be linked to the strike."

Chapter 7

Ardie responded with a groan of her own. "We all better cross our fingers and hope this is a tempest in a teapot and Marybeth Potter turns up soon." She paused and squinted at me. "Do you think Dave is involved in looking for her?"

"Maybe."

"Would he tell you if he was?"

"Maybe."

"And maybe not," Mrs. B said with a silvery laugh. "Dave's become quite stingy about sharing information about his cases. He'd tell Barbara only if he thought it would prevent her from taking action on her own."

That statement was too true for me to be annoyed about. Still, I scowled anyway. It's important to keep in practice.

"I'm surprised Dave hasn't put a tracking application on your phone," Mrs. B teased.

The truth was he'd thought of it after Allison put one on hers as part of a trust-building plan. Sure, when he brought it up he'd been crafty, suggesting we outfit all our phones as safety measures in case a situation arose where one of us was in trouble but unable to call. I saw through his scheme, however. I knew he'd leave his personal phone behind and take only the official one if he was out on something I'd find interesting. So I said I'd think about it. Since then I'd successfully danced around the topic whenever it came up.

I knew he worried about my safety—and sometimes with good reason—but having a tracker on my phone would make me feel like a kid who couldn't be trusted. And, okay, trust did come into play. Now and then I'd been guilty of avoiding a discussion of my intentions or failing to provide him with every picky little detail of what I planned to do—as if everything planned would happen as expected and nothing else would transpire.

Transparency is great. I was all in favor of it for politicians. But transparency could put a serious crimp in my style and prevent me from taking action.

Not that I could imagine any kind of action to take in this case. All I knew about Marybeth Potter was her name and her political and financial leanings. I didn't even know where she lived. Was she required to reside within school district boundaries? No matter, thanks to the Internet, I could get an address and directions in no time.

I tweaked the wrapping so tuna wouldn't cascade from between the slices of bread, and balanced the sandwich on my knee so I could work my phone. Sure, I had no plan, but collecting a few facts could pay off if—

"Stewart's getting out of his mobile office." Doug interrupted my thoughts, providing play-by-play commentary edged with sarcasm. "He's brushing crumbs from his pants. He's picking at a glop of something on his lapel. Now he's walking this way."

We all stopped chewing and watched him approach, still picking at the glop. "Sorry about spilling stuff in your car," he said to Mrs. B.

She appeared unruffled, but I knew that was due to a combination of will and acting ability. Mrs. B's car was a thing of beauty and, even while carting around my dog, friends, and booty from shopping trips, she managed to keep it in pristine condition. I noticed her sapphire eyes narrowed slightly before she spoke. "I'm sure it can be cleaned."

A more aware and socially skilled person would have offered to clean it himself or pay for a service, but Stewart wasn't that person. If Mrs. B was a 10 on a scale of empathy, sympathy, and etiquette, Stewart was somewhere below a zero. Far below a zero.

My friend Paulette once said he'd been raised by wolves. But I'd pointed out if wolves took him in as an infant, they would have driven him out of the pack when it became obvious he didn't work and play well with others. I suggested he'd been raised by busy or uninvolved parents, or by those also without the skills he lacked and without desire to cultivate them. Still, his aggressive, persistent, and often uncaring manner made him a top-notch reporter. As for the rest, I doubted he cared whether he ever got invited to formal dinner parties. I did once wonder what his dating life was like, but the queasy feeling resulting from such wondering cured me of further imaginative forays.

"Sure. Probably," he responded to Mrs. B in an offhand manner.

Her eyes narrowed again, and then she turned to me. "I believe I'll be running along, dear. I'll collect the little prince and take him with me to Verna's storage locker to pick up a few things."

I blinked.

When our friend and neighbor Verna suffered a stroke a few months ago, we'd discovered she was a hoarder. Knowing she couldn't recover and get physical therapy in a condo packed to the ceiling with what we categorized as junk, we trucked most of it off to a storage locker. When it turned out the stroke wiped Verna's memory of collecting, Mrs. B feared the loss might be temporary and kept up payments on the locker. But, as time passed and Verna made no mention of her stored possessions, we'd started to kick around ideas for disposing of what we'd crammed in there.

"Did I hear that correctly?"

"You heard completely correctly. I've been thinking there might be a few items we could use to prime the pump if we have a slow day on the air. And I need to survey what's there and trash a few things for the sake of safety. When I went by last month to check I found the decorative candles were mere puddles of wax. And with all the heat since then I'm worried about those boxes of paper and old clothing bursting into flame."

I had a sense of impending doom—and not only about spontaneous combustion. Verna's memory might return. She might realize what was missing from her condo and be furious about our interference.

As if she read my mind, Mrs. B said, "Her desire to, uh, over-collect hasn't returned yet. I'm beginning to doubt it will."

"You better be hoping while you're doubting."

She waved my concerns aside. "If there's fallout, I'll deal with it. Don't you fret."

(For the record, fretting is one of the things I do best. Having her tell me not to worry had about as much effect as me telling Dave's teenage daughter not to slam the door to her bedroom. What Mrs. B does best, however, is deal with problems of all sizes and people of all types. So I figured I'd let her worry about Verna and thus reserve fretting energy for the future of the swap show and how I might paint myself out of the picture before long. Producing had been a nice diversion and source of income over the summer. But did I want to be tied down every Saturday. For six months? For a year? For longer?)

Again, as if reading my mind, Mrs. B said, "We'll talk about Verna and the swap show—and many other things—later. When we have a few quiet moments."

The way she said "other things" made it clear one topic would be my wedding and when and where it would happen. Since I wasn't in a hurry to have that discussion—or launch an attempt to avoid it—I was glad that quiet moments made up only a small percentage of my daily life.

With a glance at Stan Stewart that would have turned an ordinary mortal to stone—or at least gravel—she headed for the porch. The pink-cheeked woman was still cuddling my entitled mutt, feeding him nuggets of something I hoped he wouldn't urp up later. His beady little eyes were, as they say, bigger than his stomach. What he gobbled down often came up—almost always on the carpet.

I suspect there's some cosmic law that makes it illegal for a dog to throw up on tile or linoleum or anywhere outside. When the urge strikes, every dog I've ever known heads straight for the nearest carpet and delivers in a centrally located spot or high-traffic area. I also suspect there's some kind of a reward system for dropping the payload while their owners are urging them toward the door. And there must be bonus points for hitting multiple spots. And for timing the "eruption" for a day when the supply of paper towels is running low.

With all that in mind, I decided to stick with the protest until the end and dawdle on the way home. That would increase the chances that Cheese Puff would drop his carpet bomb at Mrs. B's condo instead of mine.

Mrs. B gave me a fingertip wave as she passed by with Cheese Puff in her arms. He gave me a smug look that said luck wouldn't be a factor in what might transpire later.

Wondering how much remained in my spray bottle of spot treatment, I watched her unfold a couple of paper napkins and place them on the driver's seat. Then I tuned in to what Stewart was saying—in a steadily rising voice that implied he was repeating himself and getting tired of it. "All I can tell you is she's still missing, no one has any idea where she might be, and the board meeting has been postponed until later today."

"You were on the phone long enough to pass on a year's worth of state secrets," Doug said. "How can you claim that's all you know?"

"Give it up." Gertrude settled beside Doug with her sandwich. "It's not all he knows, but it's all he'll tell us."

Stewart smiled like a cat spotting a naïve canary beside a puddle of spilled cream. He shot me a wink.

I refrained from shooting him a finger but, adult that I am, stuck out my tongue as he strolled toward his car.

"Why postpone the board meeting?" Brenda asked as she raised the top slice of whole wheat bread and peered at the filling in her sandwich with a disdainful frown. I guessed her expression indicated the turkey was garnished with the usual extras and without essence of octopus or fermented carrot tops. “They have a quorum without her.”

“Maybe they need all five members for a financial decision of this magnitude,” Ardie said.

“Or maybe they feel it’s a sensitivity kind of thing,” Doug speculated. “Maybe they don’t want it to seem like they rushed to a decision without her while she’s . . .”

We exchanged glances, mentally filling in the missing word or words. Dead? Trapped in her crashed car in a ravine? Held hostage? Being brainwashed? In a coma?

Brenda’s phone rang, emitting a sound like an oven timer on steroids. She set her sandwich aside and wiggled over on one hip in order to dig it from the back pocket of her tight shorts. The pocket didn’t give up easily, and it was a long moment before she got the phone loose and answered.

“Where were we?” Gertrude asked. “Oh, wait, we were on the subject of sensitivity.” She turned to me. “Marybeth Potter would be the first to criticize them if they acted this afternoon. Of course, that’s her nature. She’s long on criticism and short on constructive ideas.”

“Sounds like the other board members might be afraid of her,” I speculated.

“Afraid might be too strong a word,” Ardie said. “But if you sit in on the meetings—and I have—there are times when you can almost feel the air get thick with tension and hear the stress meter ticking upward. She never lays into them in public, but I bet they have some behind-closed-doors sessions where the paint on the walls blisters.”

"My money says they'll kick the decision can down the road as long as possible," Gertrude said. "They'll make an announcement about thoughts and prayers, and they'll say it wouldn't be sensitive or prudent to make an immediate decision."

"The union probably won't like it," Ardie said. "But pushing for a quick vote would make for bad press."

"And we don't need that," Doug agreed.

"What about if we go on picketing?" Brenda waggled her phone. "Will we get bad press from that? Because I think we should stop. It's hot and drivers are cranky and I have things to do for Jake."

Chapter 8

"Jake?" I asked. "Jake as in my ex-husband?"

(For the record, let it be noted that, in my opinion, there was surprise but not a trace of jealousy in my tone. Escaping from the financial and emotional black hole of my short marriage to Jake Stranahan had been one of the best things I'd ever done for myself. I might feel sorry for any woman who would cozy up to him, but never would I experience even the faintest twinge of envy. Although I did reserve the right to wonder—just a little—why Jake called Brenda and exactly what their meeting would entail. And, no, I'm not going to speculate. But don't let that stop you from exercising your imagination until you learn more.)

"You have a date with Jake?" Ardie asked. Her tone was light on surprise and heavy on disbelief with a dollop of disgust.

"You don't think that's a little inappropriate?" Gertrude asked. "Jake having once been married to Barbara and all."

"That was years ago. And we don't have a date." Brenda patted her hair, the broken and uneven strands still faintly chartreuse due to a color job gone awry. "He's launching a new feature for his show and what he had planned for the first day fell through."

The second part of that statement didn't surprise me. But the first part did. Deming Featherstone hadn't mentioned anything about a new feature at the last radio station staff meeting. And, being all about forward-thinking, organizing, and leaving little to chance, he would have.

A new feature.

The words burned across my brain at the same time my blood ran cold at the use of the word "planned" in reference to Jake. First, because planning was a foreign concept to Jake. Sure, he could plan where to take a potential conquest for dinner, but he wasn't equipped to handle more detailed planning involving careful consideration of all possible outcomes and impacts. Second, because of a track record that read more like a rap sheet than a list of accomplishments, Dario had made it clear that Jake's ideas for guests and features and all proposed deviations from the norm must be presented in writing for his stamp of approval. Jake's talking skills were smooth and slick, but his writing skills were stunted and sketchy, so the requirement had kept most of Jake's schemes from landing on Dario's desk. But apparently my ex had tired of seldom getting a stamp of approval and made an end run.

"What kind of a new feature?" Ardie asked in a strangled voice.

Brenda waggled her phone again. "One that's never been done on the radio here before. He called me because I have the expertise necessary to pull it off on such short notice. And because he heard I was spontaneous."

"As in combustion," Doug muttered.

"What *is* this feature?" Gertrude's tone implied she'd be sorry she asked, but couldn't help herself.

"It's called 'Let's Bake with Jake' and it's about original recipes and adventurous baking with unusual ingredients," Brenda burbled.

"Unusual and toxic ingredients," Doug muttered.

"Every Monday he'll have a famous chef come to the radio station and whip up something, live on the air."

I did a quick mental inventory of the radio station kitchen—two square feet of counter space, a sink barely large enough to rinse out a pair of socks, and one medium-sized microwave with a balky and chipped carousel and a mind of its own when it came to counting down the seconds. There was also a coffeemaker with the habit of turning itself off in the middle of the brewing process, and a refrigerator that, despite soap, bleach, and Mrs. B's best efforts, smelled like the bottom of a bait bucket during a heat wave. An upgrade was months away.

How Jake thought that would suffice as a staging area for a cooking program was beyond me.

But then, how Jake thought—about anything other than his appearance, sex, and money—was also beyond me. His mind worked in mysterious ways. When it worked at all.

"I forgot. I got so excited I forgot." Brenda waggled the phone a third time. "Jake asked me to keep this a secret. He wants to surprise his producer. He said he wants to prove he's, um, capable of originating and implementing ideas on his own."

I groaned inwardly. Almost every previous idea Jake originated and implemented had resulted in chaos. Or an arrest. Or both. And this time he was teaming up with Brenda, the queen of nauseating cuisine.

I made a mental note to alert Deming Featherstone, Dario, the fire department, and local urgent care facilities. I made another mental note to have Mrs. B check the insurance policy and consider raising the amount of coverage on the radio station building and personnel.

"So I'm taking off now." Brenda stood and brushed grass clippings from her legs. She handed her sandwich to Doug. "You can have this. It's bland and unoriginal and I want to lose five pounds by Monday. Besides, I don't have time to eat. I need to create a recipe, buy supplies, get my hair done, have a facial, and get a manicure."

"You do know no one can see you on the radio, don't you?" Gertrude asked.

"Certainly." Brenda huffed. "But people will see me on the drive over there. And in the parking lot while I'm unloading my supplies."

"But it will be dark when you get there," I said. "Jake's show goes on the air early."

"I know that," Brenda responded. "It starts at 6:00."

And, while Jake himself breezed in only moments before that time, Deming turned out by 5:00 to update information on the day's topics, change or add questions for discussion, run sound checks with Op, and generally make sure things would proceed smoothly—or as smoothly as things could with Jake's hands on the wheel. Surely though, even a man as unconcerned about details as my ex would realize his guest chef required time to set up her equipment and walk through the format for the segment.

Or would he?

"What time did Jake tell you to be there?" I asked, trying to sound offhand.

"Uh." Brenda glanced at her phone and frowned. "He didn't say."

I bit back a laugh.

"But he told me I'd be on after the news and some talk about taxes or politics or other things he said were really boring. So I'm guessing around 7:00 or so."

My career as a radio producer hadn't been a long one, but it had been characterized by the necessity of adhering to a schedule. That meant instructing guests to arrive at the studio well before their interview slots, and stressing the importance of giving clear and concise answers because the host needed to hit specific times for commercials and station IDs. The words "or so" hadn't been included in my training.

So, as you can imagine, I was appalled, aghast, and alarmed by Jake's cavalier attitude toward planning and preparation. It was clear he'd learned nothing in the months he'd been on the air. It was also clear he knew nothing about cooking and the time necessary for measuring, mixing, and baking.

But, who was I to rain on Brenda's parade? Especially if that parade was headed along the road to what I expected would be an on-air experience that might rival the turkey drop episode of that late 70s TV show *WKRP in Cincinnati*. So I played it cool. "Well, don't worry about it. He can't start the segment until you get there, can he?"

Brenda considered for a moment. "No?"

Gertrude gaped.

Doug snickered.

Ardie cleared her throat and said, "Of course he can't." She made a brushing motion with both hands. "Now go on and take care of your preparations. I know you'll come up with a recipe that's memorable."

"Like the sinking of the Titanic was memorable," Doug muttered as Brenda scurried off, listing left and right on her high heeled sandals. "Memorable like the bombing of Pearl Harbor. Like the day Custer—"

"We get it," Gertrude said.

"We wish we didn't," Ardie added. "But we get it."

And with that we dispersed, the teachers to confer with union representatives about their course of action, and me to confer with Deming Featherstone. It was the kind of conferring best done face to face, so I drove to the downtown coffee shop Deming frequented. I had no doubt he'd be there today, pecking away at his laptop, keeping up with the news, trolling for talk topics for Jake's show, and casting lascivious glances at a perky blond barista named Meggin.

After an over-caffeinated episode that sent him to the emergency room in June, he'd limited himself to decaf after lunch. Today he was nursing something slushy and the color of caramel. Condensation beaded the outside of the clear plastic cup and made a growing puddle on the tiny table. He leaned on his elbows with his chin in his hands and his face just inches from his computer screen.

"Hey," I called. "Anyone know where I can get a decent cup of coffee in this town?"

He laughed and pulled out the vacant chair at his favorite table—the one in the rear by the restrooms. It was the last choice of everyone else and therefore nearly always available. And, while it was some distance from the counter, it gave him a good angle of sight, an angle that let him gaze upon the barista he'd fallen for. "It's on me. Coffee? Tea? A soft drink? Italian soda? Scone? Cookie?"

"Iced coffee," I blurted before he reeled off the entire menu. "Decaf. That's all."

"Plain coffee?" His tone combined shock with incredulous disbelief. "Just coffee? Only coffee."

"Coffee with a little milk."

His expression implied I'd uttered heresy or blasphemy or possibly committed treason. "No chocolate or vanilla or caramel syrup? No whipped cream?"

I sighed and sat. This was, after all, a coffee shop, a veritable shrine to roasted beans and the customers their aroma and taste enslaved. And it was, after all, located in the Pacific Northwest, the spawning bed of what they call the coffee culture. "You decide. Surprise me."

"I will." He picked up his half-empty drink. "And I'll get a fresh one while I'm there."

I watched him toddle up to the counter, wearing a goofy smile. He tugged his T-shirt lower and then pulled at both sides in an attempt to stretch the fabric so it draped rather than embraced the junior roll of flab hanging over his belt. The roll wasn't large enough yet to be called a paunch, but in another week it might be. If he didn't cut back on the sweet drinks, or if he and Meggin didn't start engaging in more aerobic activities on their dates, he'd soon be shopping for larger jeans. He might even find himself in the market for the menswear equivalent of a girdle.

(For the record, I've never worn a girdle and never shopped for one, so I have no idea what the process might involve. But I can tell you that if it includes someone unrolling a tape measure and winding it around my hips,

I'm out of there. I'll admit to carrying 10 extra pounds, but no way is anyone getting a peek at the exact distance around my hips. Granted, it's far smaller than the distance around the track at Churchill Downs or the circumference of the average Ferris wheel, but still . . .)

As I watched Deming place his order in a way that fell just short of out-and-out canoodling with Meggin, I debated how to tell him about Jake's plans. Should I take the break-it-to-him-gently approach? Or the rip-the-bandage-off-fast approach?

I decided that, having worked with Jake for five months now, Deming probably rose every morning expecting an ax of some size and sharpness to fall, if not on his neck, then somewhere in his vicinity. So, when he returned with my drink—something purplish he proclaimed was a huckleberry Italian soda—I snatched the plastic cups from his hands, set them on the table to prevent spillage should there be a severe physical reaction to the news, and dumped the cat from the bag. "Jake's gone rogue. He's booked a cooking segment for Monday morning."

Chapter 9

Deming sagged, staggered, and then sat with all the grace of an arthritic hippo parking itself on a milking stool. "Cooking?"

"Not only cooking, but cooking with the Captain Meriwether High School food and fitness teacher."

"The one who's infamous for her eel Alfredo?"

"Right. Brenda Waring."

"The one who gave herself food poisoning?"

"Right again."

"And she'll be cooking in the kitchen at the radio station?"

"Precisely."

"The kitchen without a stove or an oven?"

"Yes, the kitchen with just enough workspace to chop a stunted stick of celery with a penknife."

Deming clasped his hands on the back of his neck and thumped his head on the table. His laptop shimmied toward the edge. I released the drinks and blocked it.

"I know I'm getting experience," he moaned. "And I know the ratings are going up. I know I should be happy, but I'm so tired of trying to hold back the rising tide of insanity. I feel like that little kid who stuck his finger in the levee or dam or whatever it was. And the water keeps getting colder and higher and pushing harder. And I can't feel my finger. And . . . I really can't feel my fingers. And my arm is numb."

He sat up straight, eyes widening, and thrust his hands into the air. "I'm having a heart attack."

I shoved back my chair and stood. "Which arm is numb?"

"This one." He rubbed his left arm.

From what I'd heard and read, that wasn't good.

"No, it's this one." He rubbed the right.

That might be less bad.

"No, it's both of them. They're both numb."

I don't know a lot about medicine, but I have a lot of experience with stress and its physical manifestations. And, given that Deming was the excitable sort, probably over-sugared, possibly over-caffeinated despite his self-imposed limitation, and working with my ex on a regular basis, a little triage might be in order before I called 911.

I gripped his hands. Both were icy. Not a good sign. But he'd been holding his chilled drink and mine. And before that he'd had his arms bent and his elbows planted on the table for who knew how long. And now he had them raised above his head. "How far does the numbness go?"

"To my elbows."

"But no farther?"

He shook his head.

"Is your chest tight?"

"Yes." He gaze shifted to Meggin who had come out from behind the counter and was standing a few feet away, twisting a towel in her hands. "No. Maybe. I don't know," he sputtered. "Maybe not."

I laid two fingers beneath his jaw. His pulse was steady and strong. "Can you take a deep breath?"

"I'll see." He sucked in a couple of shallow breaths and then a deeper one. "There. How was that?"

Meggin smiled encouragement but kept twisting the towel.

"Did that hurt?" I asked Deming.

Never taking his eyes off Meggin, he pondered for a few seconds. "No."

"Good." I pulled my phone from my pocket. "I'll call for help right now if you want, or you can lower your arms, shake them a little, and see how that feels."

He hesitated, then lowered and shook, hands flapping like mittens pinned to a clothesline in a stiff breeze. "Whoa. My hands are tingling. What does that mean?"

"Your blood circulation is improving."

"That's good?"

"Yes. Take a few more deep breaths."

Meggin smiled. "Who's my widdle stressed-out bunny?" She stepped forward, leaned in, and gave him a kiss that seemed designed to make his toes tingle—along with other parts of his anatomy.

"Me," Deming gasped when she loosened the lip lock. "I'm your widdle bunny."

Good gravy.

I turned aside and took a long pull at my drink. Don't get me wrong, I'm all for love at any age. And I don't mind an occasional short and non-pornographic public display of affection. But listening to baby talk felt like listening to fingernails scrape along a chalkboard.

Looking everywhere but at Deming and Meggin, I took another pull at my drink. It wasn't the iced coffee I'd intended to have, but it was tasty. And refreshing.

After a little whispering and a smacker of a kiss I suspected people out on the street could hear, Meggin sashayed past and took up her post behind the counter.

"All better?" I asked Deming as I sat.

"For now." He felt his arms and took his pulse at the wrist. "Much better. That was frightening, though. Perhaps I should try not to think too much about Jake . . ."

"Good luck with that. Wrangling him is the biggest part of your job. It's pretty much the reason you have a job."

I recalled Stan Stewart told me back in June that reporters and photographers at the *Reckless River Roundup* had a pool going on when Deming would get his fill of Jake and turn in his resignation. If they had kept it up all this time, and if the cooking segment was the last straw, there would be a hefty payout for the winner. "You're not thinking of quitting, are you?"

"I think about quitting all the time." He shot me a smile filled with both longing and malice. "I think about how good it would feel to leave Jake in the dust."

"We don't have a lot of dust up here in the Northwest," I pointed out. "Except during the yearly summer rainless season."

"It's summer now. We haven't had rain for weeks. There's plenty of dust to leave Jake in." His gaze shifted to Meggin. "But there are reasons to hang on."

"Romance can make it easier to get through the tough stuff," I agreed.

"Definitely. And the money's good—in fact it's better than good. Plus, Dario and Mrs. B give me lots of support in other ways. They're always telling me I'm doing a great job, and they pick up my tab at the sandwich shop. And here."

He took a couple of healthy sips from his drink and saluted Meggin with his cup. "I shouldn't complain. I've got it better than a lot of people."

"Except for the part where you have to work with Jake."

"Except for that." He drew in a breath through gritted teeth. "I know I'll be sorry I asked, but what else do you know about this cooking show?"

I unloaded all I knew, then filled in more background on Brenda and explained I more than shared his doubts about the suitability of the radio station's kitchen.

"Do they make portable stoves and ovens?" he asked.

I shrugged. "I never thought about it."

"Can you bake in a microwave?"

Like medicine, cooking wasn't my area of expertise, but I hazarded a guess. "I think you can bake a few things. All I use mine for is heating up leftovers."

"Could you make a soufflé? A cherry pie? A chocolate cake? Apple strudel?"

I shrugged once more. "Probably not in that microwave."

He locked his fingers and prepared to thump his head on the table again. I jammed my palm against his chin. "Thumping your head won't change Jake or any situation he created. Believe me, I know. I was married to him."

"You're right. I have to face this." He pulled his phone from his pocket and brought up the page with Jake's information. His finger hovered over the telephone icon. "Do I have to call? Could I just send him an e-mail and tell him the cooking segment is cancelled?"

"Does Jake check his e-mail often?"

"If you define 'often' as once a week." He rubbed his temples. "Guess I have to call."

"You could pass the hot potato to Dario," I suggested.

Joy flickered in his eyes. Then the flame went out. "No. It's my job. I'll call Jake and tell him to cancel the segment."

"Wait." I seized his wrist. "Can you do that without mentioning my name? I don't mind if Jake gets bent out of shape. He can't hold a thought, but he can't hold a grudge, either. But Brenda hangs on to resentment the way barnacles stick to a boat."

If carrying that grudge involved not speaking to me, I wouldn't mind. But she'd display her wrath in other ways, ways that involved making my lunching life miserable by concocting dishes emitting odors reminiscent of a sewage lagoon. And that meant others would suffer as well.

Deming considered my request and winced. "Jake struggles to walk while he chews gum, but I think he'll wonder how I knew about his plans."

"Tell Jake you got a call from someone wanting to confirm the new segment," I suggested.

"What do I say if he asks who called?"

"Tell him you didn't get the name. Or say you had a bad connection. Or—I don't know—claim the caller wanted to remain anonymous."

He mulled that with pinched lips. Then he grinned and lifted his cup to take a sip. "Think Jake knows what 'anonymous' means?"

"Yeah. A program for mice with drinking problems."

Deming snorted his coffee drink. "Good one."

"There were others around when Brenda spouted off," I told him. "Someone might have overheard. Or maybe she called a few friends and one of them called someone who called someone who called you."

He frowned, not buying it.

"It's possible. You know how word gets around in this town. And if you throw enough 'someones' into the explanation, Jake might get confused."

"Probably." He scrunched up his eyes. "Okay. I'll call him."

But as his finger moved closer to the icon, the dark side of me took control. "Or you could forget I told you any of this."

Deming's facial expressions ran the gamut of emotions from doubt to jubilation to fear to dismay to pleasure to terror. "The show would be a disaster," he whispered.

"Pretty much," I agreed.

Another range of emotions flickered across his face. "It wouldn't be responsible of me to let that happen."

I nodded and sipped my drink.

"But it might teach Jake a lesson," he mused. "What if I compromised? What if I let Op know he should prepare for weirdness beyond the ordinary stuff? What if you let Brenda know the kitchen isn't well-equipped? What if you suggested she precook as much as she could at home?"

Since Brenda might accuse me of being jealous of her working with Jake, I wasn't wild about making that call. But in the spirit of helping Deming teach my ex a lesson, I agreed. "Works for me."

Deming laughed. "Of course it works for you. You'll be miles away on Monday. You probably won't even tune in."

"Oh, I'll definitely tune in." I stood to leave, taking the rest of my soda for the road. "I'll set my alarm. I wouldn't miss it for the world."

Chapter 10

When I got home I found Allison and Josh on the sofa. He had a giant paperback open close to his face so she couldn't see what was on the pages. She was hunched over with her hands pressed to the sides of her head. "Say the word again," she instructed.

"Unmitigated." Josh paused slightly after each syllable.

"Does it mean a fence without a gate?" Allison guessed.

I turned toward the kitchen to hide a grin.

"No," Josh said in a serious tone.

"Okay, how about someone who doesn't have mittens?"

To cover a laugh, I turned on the faucet full blast and filled a glass.

"No." Josh's voice cracked slightly on the single syllable.

Allison groaned. "Does it have something to do with the story we had to read last year? Does it mean you're not like the guy who was always imagining he had adventures when he really didn't go anywhere or do anything?"

I turned to see that Allison had stopped squeezing her temples and pressed her hands together as if in prayer. "You know the guy I mean. They made it into a movie but it was kind of different."

"Right. The story is 'The Secret Life of Walter Mitty' and that's an interesting guess," Josh said with a straight face. "But that's not what the word means."

She pounded the sofa cushions. "Then what does it mean?"

"It means 'complete' or 'absolute' and you'd use it as an adjective."

"Like if I said trying to cram stuff into my brain for the SAT is turning out to be an unmitigated disaster?"

"That's correct usage." Josh flushed. "But I wouldn't go that—"

"I would." Allison shut Josh down with a glare and a pout and tugged at her sun-streaked brown hair. "I'll never get a decent grade on the exam. I'll never go to college. I'll have to live here for the rest of my life."

Uh oh.

Josh hit me with the kind of pleading expression you might see on the face of a kid watching a nurse preparing to administer a flu shot with a needle longer than his arm, dull, and rusty. Clearly it was time for an adult to step in and deliver a pep talk.

Unfortunately, Mrs. Ballantine was nowhere in sight.

Neither was Dave.

That meant it was time to act my age.

(For the record, that's somewhere a little south of 40. Further for the record, I decline the opportunity to provide an exact number. I doubt such a right to decline is included in the Constitution—unless you stretch a few interpretations—but I'll continue to fudge on the age issue until I'm threatened with legal action, jail, or both.)

"If you believe you'll tank the SAT, then it's more likely you will." I sat beside Allison and patted her shoulder, noting as I did that she'd appropriated the turquoise T-shirt with the glittery peacock on the front Mrs. B gave me a few weeks ago. I'd tried it on, discovered it was a little tight, and put it aside for the day I lost a few pounds and it didn't encase me like the skin of a sausage. Granted, odds were the day wouldn't arrive any time soon, but hope springs eternal—including the hope Allison would one day ask permission before she looted my wardrobe.

"Is this the believe-in-yourself speech?" she asked. "The one Dad gives me all the time?"

"Uh . . ."

"Because you guys say it so much all I hear anymore is blah-blah-blah. And it doesn't make studying any easier. Or make my grades any higher."

Good points. And from a teen not noted for her ability to make good points.

"Okay. Then I won't say it. What I'll say is I think it's terrific you signed up for the test and you're working on your vocabulary. If you tank it, you can take it again."

"And the teachers' strike may mean the fall date gets canceled," Josh chimed in. "And you'll have more time to study."

Since the test was national and since test dates were set far in advance, this was a pipe dream. But if Josh's encouraging comments kept Allison from a complete meltdown, I wouldn't correct him.

"And I bet you can take some classes at the community college whether you take the SAT or not," Josh went on.

"But probably not any fun ones," Allison moaned.

Josh shot me the pleading look again and I nodded in sympathy. Allison had always managed to get passing grades, but of the barely-over-the-line variety. And, unless she underwent a radical personality change or transplant, she wouldn't buckle down and be able to carry a full load in college. So those fun classes—electives—could be far in her academic future. And the hurdles of remedial classes in math and English would stand in her way.

"Well, there's no law that says you have to go to college," I said. "There are other programs. Like culinary school."

"Luke's going there," Josh reminded her. "He starts in a couple of days."

She clutched his arm. "But you're going to college."

Ah. The problem came into focus. She wanted to be with Josh, to do what he was doing. Because she loved him. And also because she feared he'd be seduced by the wider world he was about to enter.

He shot me another glance, this one on the road to being a wince.

I adopted the brisk, no-nonsense tone most substitute teachers master during the first few hours on the job. "Well, you'll have plenty of time to meet with your counselor this fall and work out plans for what you'll do after graduation."

Allison gave me a blank stare. I took it to mean she couldn't remember which counselor she was assigned to. I made a mental note to check. It was possible her counselor had left the district, or been part of a reshuffle over the summer. I made a second mental note to beg Gertrude to move Allison to her list. That way, during our shared lunch hour, I could stay on top of issues. I vowed to sweeten the deal with a promise to help put the Family Support Room in order at least once a month and to hit up Mrs. B for another donation for families in need.

I took the prep book from Josh, closed it, and set it on the coffee table. “I think you’ve studied enough for one day. Why don’t you go to the pool?”

“Good idea.” Josh jumped to his feet. “My trunks are in the car. Be right back.”

Allison watched him head for the parking lot with the kind of expression of sadness and longing I’ve seen at airports and train stations. “He’s gonna meet a smart girl at college,” she whispered.

No way could I tell her not to worry, because she already was. And no way could I argue convincingly that she was a smart girl because I couldn’t present traditionally accepted evidence in terms of grades and choices to back that up. So I went with fact and misdirection. “He’ll meet lots of smart girls, some of them smarter than he is. Scary smart. Scary smart and interested only in school and a successful future. Scary smart without a sense of humor. Scary smart and mean. Girls who would never volunteer with a summer program like you did and help kids put on plays.”

Allison sat up straight and combed her hair with her fingers. “I did, didn’t I? I wrote some of the plays, too.”

“You did. And you got standing ovations.” Never mind that after sitting relatively still for 15 minutes, kids would have stood for almost anything short of seconds on one of Brenda’s culinary creations.

“And I helped Sybil with the costumes and sets. I was way more help than Harvey Goodspeed.”

Who wasn't? The forcibly retired major crimes investigator for the sheriff's department excelled at helping himself at all-you-can-eat buffets. And, being a my-way-or-the-highway kind of guy, he didn't work and play well with others. Still, he'd taken to his role as "enforcer" and stuck close to Sybil. That kept her from sliding off to the nearest casino for a lengthy visit with her little friends the slot machines. And, while sticking close, he'd helped her with the theater group and counseled kids to stay on the right side of the law by sharing tales from his long career.

"Maybe I could go to a theater school," Allison mused.

Not a bad idea. But were there prerequisites? Did you have to be a certain age? Or have two years of college? "That's something you and your counselor can check out. I bet there's at least one school over in Portland."

"Portland."

She said the word with the same sense of awe and delight that I would use to mouth the name of a new kind of cheesy snack. For Allison, Portland was the ultimate place to shop and eat and take in shows. Well, at least the ultimate place within a short—depending on time of day and traffic—drive.

"If I went to school in Portland, I'd have to drive there. And Dad would get me a car, right?"

Wrong.

Thanks to a test administrator I suspected was making sure he'd never have to ride with her again, Allison had gotten a driver's license. But descriptions of her ability to operate a motor vehicle in a manner consistent with the rules of the road, still involved the use of words such as "erratic, mercurial, mindless, inattentive" and others of that ilk. Unless Dave had a lapse of judgment similar to the one Napoleon had when he decided to invade Russia, there was no way he'd allow her to drive in Portland. Generally, streets were more narrow and drivers more short-tempered than in Reckless River. Plus, getting there and back required merging onto the Interstate and I knew experienced drivers who shuddered at the thought of doing that at any hour.

And no way would Dave provide her with a car. When the subject had been raised—and it had been raised many times—he'd taken a firm position that before she got a car she needed to have a job to cover insurance, gas, and repairs.

But, not wanting to subject myself to a discussion/argument, I didn't bring up any of what was on my mind. Nor did I mention the possibilities of taking the bus or carpooling with other students.

While I tried to think of something encouraging but noncommittal, Josh returned, phone to his ear, an expression of astonishment on his face. "That mean school board lady got kidnapped."

"Seleena's mother?" Allison asked.

"Yeah. Maybe not kidnapped, but she's missing." He tapped his phone and tucked it in his pocket. "Maybe she was in an accident and has amnesia."

"Bet Seleena's crying alligator tears. Bet she goes on TV and begs for money to help search. Then spends it on shoes." Allison flopped back on the sofa and raised her feet to study a pair of green flip-flops decorated with white daisies. "She's all about shoes. But mostly all she can afford are knockoffs."

"Who's Seleena?" I asked.

"The daughter of the mean school board woman," Josh said. "I bet you had her in class. Not this year, but the one before. She was a grade ahead of me."

I squinted, thinking.

(For the record, I have no idea why I tend to squint when engaged in a deep probe of my memory banks. Maybe I have a subconscious belief that narrowing my eyes will help focus images from the past. I've also—although I know it doesn't help one bit—been known to take my glasses off and polish the lenses.)

"She's tall and has long hair," Allison prompted.

Not much help. At least half the girls at Captain Meriwether High School had long hair.

"And a bad attitude," Josh contributed.

Also not much help. Given educational requirements, economic situations, high levels of parental pressure and expectations, low levels of parental encouragement, approval, or supervision, and the nature of high school in general, bad attitudes came with the territory.

"If she was late to class and you asked why," Allison said, "she probably told you her mother was on the school board. She probably said you weren't allowed to mark her tardy."

"Like she was daring you to do something," Josh added.

Aha.

Chapter 11

The bit about daring me brought up a mental image—Seleena Potter, tossing back her shiny hair and informing me of her mother's position in a voice best described as snotty. It also resurrected a memory of me trying to come up with a response free of sarcasm and settling for zipping my lips and simply nodding. At the end of class, before I turned in the roll sheet, I'd put a big, fat T for tardy beside her name. "Now I remember."

"I knew you would," Josh said. "The annoying kids stand out."

So did the helpful and kind and smart ones. I learned their names fast and remembered their faces with ease. But the kids in the middle . . . Well, as hard as I tried, the quiet kids who didn't give me grief or shoot their hands up to respond to questions got lost in my mental shuffle. In my defense, I faced about 150 kids every day and, as you well know, I'm no rocket scientist. But I always feel I should be better at the name game. And I always feel I owe the kids in the middle a big apology.

"Nobody liked Seleena. Not even the guys," Allison said. "She was really annoying."

"She still is," Josh said. "When she comes in for lunch she acts like she owns the place. Even Lana hates to see her. She never says anything, but I can tell."

"How?" I asked. Lana Dylan, with a heart of gold and rose-tinted glasses, strove to see the best in everyone and treat all customers as if they were valued and special. "How can you tell?"

"She does this little thing when the difficult customers come in." Josh pressed his forefinger on the space between his eyebrows and drew it down about half an inch. "Like she's clicking a switch, putting herself on automatic pilot, or bringing up a shield or something."

Allison copied his motion. "Wish you could really do that. Put up a shield, I mean. I'd click the switch all the time."

Probably every time I mentioned chores that needed to be done, or whenever Dave brought up pesky subjects like homework or the state of her room.

"Let's go back to those alligator tears." I opened the refrigerator and surveyed the contents with an eye toward scavenging the makings of dinner. "You don't think she's worried about her mother?"

"She's probably more worried about losing her shoe allowance," Allison said.

"When she wasn't dropping her name to get special treatment, she was telling everyone how much she hated her mother and how she couldn't wait to graduate and get away from her and all her rules." Twirling his swim trunks on one finger, Josh headed for the tiny washroom off the kitchen. "But she never went anywhere. She's working at a discount shoe store in that ugly strip mall."

The description didn't narrow it down much. "Which ugly strip mall?"

"The one with the comics shop where the owner brings his snake to work."

Allison and I exchanged similar looks of revulsion. There were many things we didn't agree on, but the topic of snakes always found us on the same page.

"It's kind of near the sandwich shop," Josh added.

That brought up a mental image of the place. With the image came a few descriptive and unflattering adjectives.

"The snake is really big," he said with a touch of awe. "And yellow."

I shuddered and made a mental note to avoid passing the strip mall if possible and speed up if I couldn't.

"And Seleena is still living at home."

Allison made claws with her hands. "You say you don't like her, but you know a ton about her."

Josh made a calm-down gesture. "I know about the job because while she was counting out change for her sandwich, she complained about her manager, her hours, her pay, and how the discount she gets on shoes is worthless because the shoes are all a year behind the trends. And I know she's still at home because one time she called and wanted us to deliver to her mom's house."

Allison's fingers curved farther. "And did you?"

"Heck, no. First, the order was too small. And second, her address was outside our delivery area."

Allison's hands relaxed. "Bet she was—"

"Totally." Josh grinned and closed the washroom door.

Allison turned to me. "I would have caught myself before I said a word I'm not supposed to use. Honest. I would have."

I doubted that, but nodded. In an effort to help her get employment-ready, Dave and I had insisted language used in our presence should be family-friendly. And I mean the kind of family that doesn't get together to make X-rated movies or teach sailors how to swear.

"Gonna put my suit on." Allison headed for the stairs.

"And put my T-shirt back in my dresser where it belongs?"

"You never wear it," she whined.

"That's not the point."

She paused for a moment, only her legs still in view, and then tromped the rest of the way to her bedroom. Apparently her theory was that if she couldn't think of a comeback, she could always make noise. Correction, make extra noise.

As I assembled the makings of a Mediterranean salad, I thought about relationships and how difficult they could be—especially when a self-centered teen was involved. I knew next to nothing about Seleena and her mother, but it seemed their relationship was especially prickly. Seleena didn't like the restrictions her mother placed upon her, but she liked using her mother's power. She didn't like living at home, but she liked the financial benefits and the clothing and shoes her mother provided.

Did those expensive shoes come with an emotional price tag? Were they, in essence, leashes keeping Seleena close to home and displaying some degree of gratitude and occasional brief demonstrations of affection? Were they badges signifying Marybeth's success selling real estate? And how did the woman who voted for cuts justify pampering her daughter? By claiming her case was different? Or by blocking deep thought on the matter?

Having blocked deep thought on a number of matters—such as what my craving for cheesy snacks said about my life and the emotional holes I was trying fill—I knew how easy it could be to get in the habit of sidestepping. And, as you well know, I've also been accused of believing in the presence of small print reading "Except for Barbara Reed" on the bottom of signs and beneath paragraphs of regulations. So, although I didn't view Marybeth Potter as someone I could welcome to my circle of friends, and although I couldn't defend her position on school funding issues, I bet she had wounds in her past. So I felt sorry for her. Not really, really, really sorry. But a tiny smidge sorry. A really tiny smidge. More like a smidge of a smidge.

"Thanks for letting me hang out here," Josh said as he emerged in a pair of blue and green swim trunks. They were loose and boxy enough to hide half a dozen bags of potato chips or a couple of puppies.

Not wanting to appear as ignorant of fashion trends as I was, I went on slicing cucumber and didn't ask whether this was the style. "No problem."

"Really," he said in a serious tone. "Thanks for helping me out all the times you have. And for trusting me. You and Mr. Martin are the greatest. You're like my second parents."

I set the knife aside. Slicing while tearing up was a good way to nick a finger. "You're pretty great yourself, Josh. Dave and I hope that . . ."

I paused before I stumbled into a minefield.

Josh helped me out. "Whatever happens with Allison we can stay in touch?"

"Yes. And remain friends."

He stuck out his hand. "You bet."

"Deal." We shook and I followed up with a hug. He returned it with interest.

When I first met him, Josh was a junior at Captain Meriwether. He'd been a stringy kid with long hair and a guitar he carried with him everywhere. In two years he'd added weight and muscle and chopped off his hair. "Do you still play the guitar?"

"Yeah. But not every day." I released him and he shrugged. "Got the job at the sandwich shop. Had to get serious about studying and college."

"Promise me you won't give it up entirely. Music will stimulate your brain and fill you up when other things are draining you."

As if on cue, Allison thudded downstairs, jumping from step to step.

"Enjoy the pool," I said in a bright voice.

"Thanks again," Josh called over his shoulder as he hurried to join her on the way to the door.

"Why are you thanking her?" Allison asked. "What were you talking about?"

"Nothing much," Josh mumbled. "College and stuff."

"What kind of stuff?" Allison persisted as they let themselves out. "Stuff about me? It was, wasn't it? It was about me."

"Keep that guitar tuned, Josh," I muttered as I returned to the cucumber. "Don't misplace your pick."

Chapter 12

I was tossing walnuts on top of the salad when Dave came in wearing the expression of weary accomplishment he'd sported since Harvey Goodspeed finally left the building and stopped telling him how the job should be done. Today's version, however, involved less brow furrowing and more gleam in warm brown eyes that reminded me of milk chocolate or maybe coffee with just a dash of cream.

"You look like a man who spotted the light at the end of the tunnel."

"Finally." He bent to kiss my left temple before he pulled a bottle of beer from the refrigerator and twisted off the cap. "And it appears to be daylight and not an oncoming train." He inspected the salad as he drank. "Just nuts? No meat?"

I slid the bowl into the refrigerator. "You had meat for lunch."

"You don't know that." He took a step back and narrowed his eyes. "How do you know that?"

"I don't. It was a lucky guess based on previous knowledge of midday meals consisting of burgers, roast beef sandwiches, and sausage pizza." I tapped his chest. "And then you gave yourself away."

"How?"

I mulled my answer for a few seconds. It wouldn't do to let Dave know I was aware of all his tells. But this reaction had been so obvious he was liable to figure it out for himself. "First, you adopted a defensive attitude. You stepped back and squinted. And second, you had a certain wariness in your voice when you asked how I knew."

"Got to work on that." He slumped to the sofa. "So, I get meat only once a day?"

"Given the usual size of the meat portions you devour, once a day probably supplies all the protein you need." I carried the olive oil to the pantry. "But I'm betting you also had meat for breakfast. So that's twice today."

The flush that crept up his cheeks was visible through his stubble. "Ham and cheese and egg biscuit," he mumbled. "Man can't live on a breakfast of oatmeal and fruit and yogurt."

"Man can if he wants to trim his bad cholesterol level."

Dave snorted and kicked off his shoes—leather shoes. The job called for a higher-class wardrobe than he'd worn when he was a drug cop in the Reckless River Police Department. Then he'd been all about worn running shoes, ragged jeans, and T-shirts that appeared to be a day away from becoming dust rags. Now it was khaki slacks and shirts with collars and sleeves. And now he tucked those shirts in when he put on one of the two jackets he possessed. He even—courtesy of Mrs. B—owned a tie. He had yet to wear it.

I got to work wiping down the countertops. "Have you gone through all the files?"

When Harvey Goodspeed's health forced his retirement, he hadn't gone without a fight—and without trashing the office and scattering years' worth of paper case files. Once he'd straightened things out, Dave had been working on his own time, evenings and Saturdays, to review details and enter pertinent data into the system.

He had a new computer to do the entering. Harvey had broken the old one. Prior to that, he'd treated the keyboard more as a paperweight and/or placemat than a means of storing, collating, and retrieving data.

"I'm almost through the last box. And I would have had that finished if your sister hadn't called three times to insist I get to work on what she refers to as 'her' project."

"She called me once to nag you to get on it."

"Only once?"

"Yes. She also threatened to come by, but I told her I'd be on the picket line all afternoon and she could join me if she had something important to say."

Dave grinned. "Well played. Thank you for not nagging me."

"No problem. If I'm going to prod and provoke, it will be for something on my agenda, not hers."

Not that prodding—even in less-than-subtle ways—had much effect. Provoking, on the other hand, got quick results. Not always better results, but I took what I could get.

"Did you picket all afternoon?"

"No. I was there only a little while when we got word that Marybeth Potter was missing." I tossed the sponge in the sink and studied him, watching for a tell if he tried to fib. "Are you involved in the search?"

"There's no search. She's an adult. She's overdue for a meeting."

"She's a woman who sticks to a schedule like lobbyists stick to politicians. No way would she miss a chance to vote against the union unless she was tied up at the bottom of an abandoned mineshaft."

Dave cocked his head. "Do we have abandoned mines around here?"

"I don't know. But that's not the point. Something or someone kept her from making that meeting. She wouldn't have skipped it to spend the afternoon at a spa."

"All supposition." He peeled off his socks, planted his heels on the coffee table, and wiggled his toes. "Anyway, city police have the lead on this, and until they decide she's officially missing there's no official search."

"Does that mean there's an unofficial search?"

Dave sipped his beer, an act that told me he was buying time, not savoring the contents of the bottle. The first beer on a hot day was a thirst quencher. The second was the one he sipped and savored.

"It means officially I wasn't working today, and officially I wasn't called in to participate in any investigation that may or may not have taken place. And it means that any suggestions I may have made were unofficial. And any discussions of the logistics of any activities related to Ms. Potter's failure to appear at the school board meeting were also unofficial."

That sounded like a lot of verbal tap dancing to me. It also sounded as if police were taking this more seriously than Dave admitted. Because of Potter's high profile? Or because they had reason to suspect foul play?

"Has her car turned up? Her purse? Anything?"

Dave examined the label on his beer bottle, but said nothing. That, I knew from past experience, was his way of telling me to give it up.

(For the record, Dave has the impression that I can't keep a secret. And, okay, there may be some grounds for that. In the past I haven't always been successful at preventing others from prying details of law enforcement activities from me. Sometimes they've done this by taking advantage of my own tells. And sometimes my desire to climb out of my rut and take off in pursuit of justice has led to some oversharing.)

"Don't get involved with this," he said.

"Involved? How would I get involved? I know almost nothing about the woman. I have no idea where to search for her."

"Maybe *you* don't, but there's a possibility some of your teacher friends might."

"How? How would they know where to look?"

He said nothing and I clicked on what he meant. "Are you saying one of them might be responsible for her disappearance? One of them might have kidnapped her? Or worse? You think Ardie or Gertrude or Doug would do something like that?"

He raised his hands. "You have to admit tempers are running high and hot."

I thought of Aston's reaction to the shrill woman cruising past the picket line. Sure, that was a hot-headed reaction. But the word "reaction" was the key. "So you jump from hot tempers to the conclusion that one of my friends—?"

"I don't think anything right now. All I'm saying is don't go off on a scavenger hunt. And especially don't go off on your own without letting me know where you're headed."

He paused a few seconds and then added "Please."

Even with that tacked on, it was still what amounted to an order. And giving me an order of any kind—except perhaps an order to check out a new brand of cheesy snack or have a second piece of cake—was like waving a cape at a bull.

But I didn't react.

I didn't argue.

And I didn't roll my eyes.

I also didn't make a promise I might break later.

Chapter 13

Marybeth Potter's disappearance made the top of the front page of the Sunday morning edition of the *Reckless River Roundup*. I read the entire article with eager anticipation while fueling up on coffee and a blueberry muffin. My quest for nuggets of real news was largely fruitless and led me through a maze of non-informational expressions. Knowing Stan Stewart as I did, I could feel a strong undercurrent of frustration beneath expressions like "awaiting word" and "no official comment." A sidebar provided a brief bio of the school board chair that turned aggressiveness and bullying into more positive attributes like determination and steadfast belief in core values.

Whatever.

Dave, wearing jogging shorts and a T-shirt with more holes than a crocheted doily, poured coffee into the largest mug in the cabinet and trudged to the sofa.

"Going running?"

"Yeah. Before it gets too hot." He flopped on the sofa, swung his bare feet to the coffee table, seized the remote with his free hand, and clicked the TV on. "Huh. Um. Wow. No way. All right."

That last comment, coupled with the absence of further clicking, the sound of the crack of a bat against a ball, and his bare feet, made me doubt he'd get out on the riverfront trail before it got too hot. If he got there at all.

I tossed my muffin wrapper in the trash can under the sink and slugged down the rest of my coffee. “Heading for the rec center. We’re putting all the summer activity stuff in storage.”

Dave waved the remote but said nothing. Not that I expected him to sacrifice his only day off to help, and not that I expected him to leap to his feet and take me in his arms for a farewell smooch that would make my toenails tingle. But blowing a kiss and adding a simple “goodbye” or a “see you later” would have been nice. Still, I wasn’t about to go all B.B. King and moan about the thrill being gone. If I opened the door to the relationship-related complaint closet, Dave would again bring up my tendency to take off on USUIE missions and put myself in danger. So I kissed the top of his head—a head covered with bed-head hair in need of a trim—and took off.

Cheese Puff had spent the night at Mrs. B’s and greeted me when I arrived at the rec center. The greeting consisted of opening his beady little eyes, lifting his head a full inch off the cushion he reclined upon at the edge of the low stage, yawning, and returning to his nap. The males in my life clearly were not falling over themselves with efforts to make me feel loved and appreciated.

My neighbors Sybil and Verna were up on the stage collecting and packing costumes and props used in the summer productions. Well, Sybil was collecting and Verna was packing. Still troubled by weakness following a stroke, she was seated on a stool, folding items from a steadily growing pile and fitting them into a large plastic tub as if wedging pieces into a three-dimensional puzzle. Her long fingers worked quickly and she glanced up only for a second and shot me a lopsided smile. Some days the side of her face compromised by the stroke worked better than others.

Lola, Dave's former canine partner, sat beside her, muzzle lifting and falling as her gaze followed each action. Perhaps because she'd been injured and walked with a limp herself, the Golden Retriever never displayed impatience or boredom.

Sybil, meanwhile, fluttered to and fro from shelves and tables at the rear of the stage, her dandelion-fluff hair lifting and falling with a breeze of her own creation. She filled her arms with wigs, scripts, and bright garments, many of which escaped her grip before she reached Verna's side.

Harvey Goodspeed trailed her, gathering what she dropped in his own way. Even if he'd wanted to muster up the energy to bend, his large belly would have made it difficult if not impossible. So his gathering involved kicking items ahead of him toward a stack of empty tubs beside Verna. He did it without much care.

I was certain Verna noticed, and just as certain she'd decided to say nothing. Thanks to Harvey's vigilance, Sybil's addiction to gambling appeared to be in the past. We were all grateful for that. What we weren't so grateful for was Sybil's infatuation with Harvey. But there was nothing any of us could do—legally, at least.

Mrs. Ballantine rushed past lugging a long and narrow plastic box. As she disappeared through the door to a patio she called, "I found the perfect container for the fishing rods. Aston, please clean all the dead worms from the hooks and wipe the poles before you pack them away."

Doug appeared through the doorway to the kitchen. "I have a feeling I'd better help with that fishing pole project." He hooked a thumb toward the kitchen. "Could you give Ardie a hand with Brenda's stuff?"

I made the finger-down-the-throat sign for gagging. What Brenda had created with her "stuff" hadn't exactly smelled like baking sugar cookies or roses in bloom when it was fresh from the stove. And it had been at least a week since she put on a cooking demonstration for kids. My stomach flipped at the thought of what I'd encounter. "She's not coming to clean up her own mess?"

Doug gawked at me as if I was trying to win the stupid-question-of-the-year award. "Has she ever cleaned her crap out of the refrigerator at school?"

I shook my head and he trucked on past saying he rested his case.

And he was correct. It was Ardie who tossed odds and ends and sanitized the small refrigerator in the teachers' room we shared. And it was the school custodians—complaining all the while about needing hazard pay—who dumped the contents of the cabinets and refrigerators in her classroom when the summer break began. Brenda seemed to feel that dreaming up recipes, assembling ingredients, and presenting "culinary masterpieces" exempted her from further effort.

Thinking about Brenda reminded me I'd agreed to call and let her know the radio station kitchen fell far short of the mark—even a mark set by someone who seldom did more in the way of cooking than nuke a slice of pizza or heat a cup of water for tea.

I punched her number on my cell and, to my relief, got a recording. "I'm sure Jake told you there's no conventional oven or stovetop burners at the radio station," I said without a trace of sarcasm or amusement, "but I know you were excited when he called, so I thought I'd make sure you didn't mishear or misunderstand. There's a microwave, but sometimes it shuts down for no reason and sometimes it doesn't turn off when it should. And counter space is limited. But you're a pro. I'm sure you and Jake will make the food, and the feature, a huge success."

That last sentence was a flat-out lie. Brenda alone might be able to cobble together something edible—or as edible as any of her creations got—but with Jake's help the odds of success diminished to the vicinity of zero.

Chortling, and grateful I had nothing more than coffee and the muffin in my stomach, I ambled to the rec center kitchen to help clean up. It was a cavernous room, designed for community use for weddings, celebrations, potlucks, and other gatherings. It featured two refrigerators, three sinks, a massive stove as well as a smaller model, two microwave ovens, an enormous dishwasher, and yards of counter space with cabinets above and below. A pass through window opened to a dining room. A set of double doors—both open—led to a patio populated by six picnic tables and a cluster of lawn chairs.

Ardie, a vision in shorts and a T-shirt—both black, in case you needed to ask—surveyed the pots and pans crammed in a row of lower cabinets. "I have no idea what Brenda brought in and what belongs to the center."

I bent to get a better view of the jumble. "She stresses that she uses only the best quality cookware, but I doubt she buys it new—at least not all of it."

"And you suspect this why?"

“I once spotted her buying a stock pot at a thrift store. It had a bent handle and it needed a good cleaning, but it was a famous brand.”

“I don’t think I could name a famous cookware brand if you threatened to paint my toenails pink.”

We both looked at her black sandals and the coat of deep purple polish on the nails of her long toes. “Is that gold glitter?” I asked.

“Yes. Trying to prove to Gertrude that I’m not so far into a rut I can’t climb out now and then.” She flexed her toes, and then swept a hand through the air to indicate it was time to work. “How about we take everything out of the cabinets, lay it on the long table against the wall, and assess what’s there?”

“Good plan.”

“You do the assessing and sorting. You’ve known Brenda longer.”

“How does that qualify me for the job?”

“You’ve seen more of her pots and pans at school.”

True. But I’d never paid much attention. “That reasoning is as weak as one-dunk-of-the-bag tea.”

“It’s all I could come up with.” Ardie showed me a grin that was more smug than apologetic. “Before we start, I’ll shut down the refrigerators. We were supposed to use only the one on the right, but I saw Brenda rooting in the other one. I’ll open the doors so they can air out some.”

I grimaced. “Won’t the stuff in there smell worse as it approaches room temperature?”

“Definitely, but that will help us identify what we’ll need to double bag to protect the sanitation workers who collect it.”

I didn't bring up the danger to feral dogs or those who regularly dug through the rec center trash in search of food or cans and bottles to recycle. After all, if we had to take our chances with Brenda's leavings, why shouldn't they?

Then I had second and more humanitarian thoughts. "How about I take the bags of really bad stuff home and toss them in the containers at the condo complex. Those are so tall no one scavenges through them."

Ardie turned from the refrigerator with an expression of awed amazement on her face. "You'd put bags of this stuff in your car?"

"In the trunk," I clarified. "And I'll drive like the wind. A really fast wind."

"A fast and stinky wind." Ardie snorted and opened the refrigerator doors. "Let's see what we've got before you commit."

With a resounding clatter, she reached into a cabinet and then dealt pot lids out like playing cards. Not to be outdone, I piled up pots and pans, including a crumb-crusted trove from a drawer beneath the stove, a water-spotted trio of saucepans from the dishwasher, and two blackened cookie sheets from the oven.

Cheese Puff, perhaps believing the sounds signaled kibble or biscuits would follow, trotted in and made a circuit of the room, sniffing at every open door. He paused at the refrigerator and put one paw on the lowest shelf. "No," I ordered in my firmest substitute teacher voice. "Outside. Find Lola."

He raised his upper lip in a look of disdain verging on a snarl.

I pointed to the door. "Find Lola."

He removed his paw and sniffed the contents of the lowest rack on the door.

"Now," I ordered.

Moving like an anemic sloth, he obeyed.

"I've thought about taking him to obedience class for a refresher course," I told Ardie by way of apology for his behavior.

"Waste of time and money," she said. "As long as his fans think he's adorable just as he is, nothing will change."

True. His fans were members of the Cheese Puff Care and Comfort Committee, a group Mrs. B started when my schedule was packed with subbing and graduate classes. Their initial goals had been to see he got regular walks and had fresh water and occasional snacks. Before long, however, they were taking him to restaurants, movies, and art galleries, and generally treating him like royalty. Mrs. B even took to referring to him as the little prince. There were plenty of weeks when I envied his social life and dining options, and plenty of days when I wondered if it was possible for him to become any more spoiled or entitled.

Ardie raised her hands. "Don't get me wrong. I like dogs. But it seems like the big ones are easier. It seems like they're more eager to please."

"Cheese Puff is eager to please," I said with a biting laugh. "Eager to please himself."

Ardie snorted once more, surveyed the pile on the long table, and grabbed the cookie tins. "I don't care if these were endorsed by the greatest chef who ever sautéed or flambéed in Paris." She stuffed them in a black plastic sack. "I wouldn't use them. Not even to slide down an icy hill or catch an oil drip under my car."

"Aston might want them to build a door for his cave."

"Let's hope he's past that. It's great he knows how to live off the land and all, and I don't want to see him become just another face in a dull and conforming crowd, but I'd like him to use more common sense." Ardie knelt and reached to the back of a cabinet to bring out an ancient grinder, a grater bent like a horseshoe, and a wooden spoon with a splintered handle. "If he keeps on pushing the envelope with Tremaine, he'll find himself without an envelope to push. And without a pay envelope as well."

I nodded, but didn't mention that she was preaching to the choir. The amusement value of Aston's antics in the name of historical reenactment in the classroom was wearing thin for Captain Meriwether Principal Tremaine Scott. I suspected he was reaching the end of a long but badly fraying rope.

"These cabinets need a major scrubbing." Ardie stood, snapped on a pair of black—naturally—rubber gloves, and got an old towel and a spray bottle of degreasing solution from a small plastic bucket. "I'll tackle that while you sort. Then we'll go through the upper cabinets."

By the time I'd sorted cookware by type and size, tossed pots that could be cleaned only with a blowtorch, and set aside what I believed might belong to Brenda, the heap was about half the original size. Ardie and I organized and stowed with care, then took deep breaths, and tackled the upper cabinets. These were filled with mixing bowls, storage containers, canned goods, spices, and sacks of flour and sugar.

When Ardie opened the first sack in line, two pantry moths flew out. She swatted them to the floor with her towel and I leaped and stomped, committing mothicide without a qualm.

"Dump, dump, dump," she ordered. "If it's not in a can or a jar or sealed up in some kind of a moth-proof container, it goes." She shook open a fresh trash bag. "I don't care if it belongs to the mayor's mother, if a moth can get in, let's assume at least one already has."

"To quote, sort of, from *Jaws*," I said, pointing at the black plastic sack. "'You're gonna need a bigger bag.'"

Ardie chuckled, seized two boxes of muffin mix and dumped them. "Never have seen that whole movie. Thought it would be too scary. But they've made far scarier flicks since then, so I guess I wouldn't be too frightened."

"Said the woman who works at a high school and is about to clean out a refrigerator full of Brenda Waring's toxic taste treats."

"The irony isn't lost on— Hey! He's stealing stuff from the refrigerator." Ardie pointed to my scruffy orange dog.

Cheese Puff froze, caught in the act of tugging a plastic bag filled with what appeared to be green slime through the open doors to the patio.

Chapter 14

"Cheese Puff. No." I dropped a box of baking soda and took off after him. "Don't eat that. Drop it. Drop it now."

With a final tug, he made it through the doors. When I reached the patio I saw that, for the first time in months, he'd obeyed and dropped the sack.

Unfortunately, Lola had picked it up.

"Lola. No. Drop it."

Lola, trained to sniff out drugs and conditioned to obey commands, ignored me. Leaving a trail of green splotches, she set off across the patio toward the outdoor sports courts.

My flip-flops slapping concrete, I gave chase. Behind me, Ardie shouted, her words indistinct. Cheese Puff barked in a way that told me his intention was clear. He was on a mission, and she stood in the way.

I left them to their skirmish and followed Lola to the horseshoe pits beyond the tennis courts. By the time I caught up, she'd deposited the sack in a hole and was shoving sand on top with her paws. Around her were half a dozen partially filled holes.

"I guess you think you're helping."

Lola wagged her feathery tail.

I knelt and hugged her, breathing in the scent of shampoo that smelled of rain and new grass. When Verna had her hair done, she dropped Lola off at a canine spa for the full treatment. Once, when she had a two-for-one coupon, she took Cheese Puff. Now, sadly, he was barred from the place, barred for the crime of inciting three other small dogs to escape from their drying cages. Once they were free, they'd tugged at leashes dangling from a bar and pulled over a display rack of canine bath products, deodorizing sprays, treats, and accessories.

Before the culprits were rounded up, one managed to bite open sample packets of treats and spread the contents. The others rolled shampoo bottles along a hallway where the owner, hurrying to check on the crash, tripped on one and sprained an ankle.

Mrs. B had tried to smooth things over with cash and the claim that Cheese Puff was simply high-spirited and hadn't intended to do damage. When the spa owner wouldn't budge, my wealthy neighbor took another approach, questioning the sound business sense of anyone who would purchase and stock treats in packets that could be torn open so easily. She followed that up by suggesting the owner needed glasses and should work on her powers of observation and balance issues.

To my secret joy and approval, the owner took the cash to cover damages, but stuck to her guns about the little prince. Thanks to the tales she passed along, Cheese Puff is also barred from two other canine spas and a third wants 50% more for a visit.

Needless to say, Mrs. B was miffed, so miffed she toyed with the idea of opening a canine spa of her own. And she was furious when Verna, whose love for Cheese Puff isn't blind, refused to boycott the spa to show solidarity.

An entire day went by before my wealthy neighbor calmed down and admitted Cheese Puff "may" have caused a few "minor" problems. But she continued to insist—even after many weeks—that he should have a second chance. The spa owner continued to refuse.

"Was this his idea?" I asked Lola.

She whined and nudged more sand into the hole with her front paws.

"I'll take that to mean it was."

She whined again and I scratched her ears. "I'm not mad. You thought you were helping. Verna's great, but her lifestyle is more sedentary than you're used to, so I bet you wanted a little activity."

Lola gave me what could have been a nod.

"At least you didn't roll in it like you did with that mess Dave cooked up a few months ago."

She barked as if to say she was past all that.

"Good. I'm glad we had this chat." I grasped her collar. "Now come with me. You're gonna hang with Verna while I dig this stuff up and bag it."

"Captured him while he was trying to drag out more." With Cheese Puff across her shoulder like a baby about to be burped, Ardie hustled past the end of the fence that enclosed the tennis courts.

"Lola's been burying what he hauled out." I pointed to the mounds.

"Think you can get her to dig the stuff up again so we don't have to?"

"Maybe. She's smart. She'd catch on fast. But I'm afraid she'd rupture a container."

"And we'd be fined by the EPA." Ardie handed over Cheese Puff. "And other agencies all the way down the line to the local health department. You take them inside and explain to Mrs. B and Verna why they're now banned from the kitchen. I'll get trash bags and rubber gloves."

When we met back at the scene of the canine crime, she had Doug in tow. He was armed with a shovel, a rake, and the latest on Marybeth Potter's disappearance.

"I was loading up my car for a run to the storage locker and the guy at the front desk told me he heard her car turned up. Not too far from the sandwich shop. Behind the all-night tanning place."

Ardie and I knew right where that was. When it opened we'd speculated about people who would turn out to toast themselves in the middle of the night. Would they be insomniacs? Those with incredibly busy schedules? Singles preparing for early coffee dates? Vampires?

"I doubt she was the tanning type," Ardie said. "She was in the business of causing wrinkles. She wouldn't want to risk calling attention to her own. Not like that woman we saw at the supermarket last week."

I snorted a laugh. When it came to tanning, the woman had been a classic overachiever. Her long hair was a silvery blond, but dry and brittle. Her skin was the color of toasted almonds, except for the tiny white lines on her face, hands, and elbows. The pale area around her eyes made her appear to be wearing goggles and gave her an expression of perpetual surprise.

Not wanting to be caught staring, we'd taken turns peering over the tops of magazines snatched from the rack by the checkout stand. Later, after examining the way our skin folded and bunched, we realized the white lines represented tiny wrinkle canyons, areas shielded from tanning rays. I wondered if the woman noticed. Then I wondered if she cared. Then I decided it wasn't my business. Maybe she even liked the look.

(For the record, if you're a sun worshipper, Southwest Washington isn't a prime place to pay homage to the yellow globe in the sky. In parts of the Pacific Northwest, that globe is shielded by clouds of various types and thicknesses for a substantial part of the year. Personally, I avoid tanning because it could cause skin cancer and may contribute to early and/or advanced wrinkling. But mostly I avoid it because it involves wearing minimal amounts of clothing and thus revealing excess skin, some of which is stretched across excess fat. Plus, tanning outside is mostly accompanied by sweating and, whenever possible, I try to avoid sweating.)

"Did they find anything in her car?" Ardie asked. "Blood? Signs of a struggle?"

"All I heard was that they found the car." Doug opened a trash bag, fitted a second one inside, and cocked his head toward me. "I bet if you called Stan Stewart you could get more."

"Not happening." I used the edge of a shovel to clear sand from Lola's most recent contribution. "I refuse to demean myself."

"What about Dave?" He needled as he held the sack open. "I bet he knows plenty."

"Maybe not. The car was found inside the city limits."

"Yeah," he persisted. "But don't they share information with the sheriff's department? Don't they have joint task forces and stuff like that?"

"Yes." Making no attempt to shake off excess sand, I scooped up the sack of slime and dumped it in the garbage bag. It hit the bottom with a squishy thud that turned my stomach. “But it could take time to set up a task force. And Dave might not be on it.”

“Of course he will.” Doug carried the bag to the mound in the next horseshoe pit. “Kidnapping Marybeth Potter is a major crime.”

“We don’t know she was kidnapped.” Ardie raked the first pit smooth. “Maybe she went off somewhere for a romantic weekend.”

Doug closed his eyes. “I don’t even want to begin to imagine the form romance with her would take. If the poor guy didn’t meet her performance goals she’d probably bite off—”

“His head?” Ardie guessed. “Like those stick insects do?”

“Praying mantises,” Doug said. “And I thought I read somewhere that isn’t a regular occurrence.”

“You could ask Aston,” I suggested.

“He wouldn’t know. You can’t shoot a praying mantis. Well, you could, but there wouldn’t be anything left to skin or skewer and roast over a fire.” Doug shook the bag. “And don’t tell me to ask Brenda or I’ll get a lecture on the protein content of insects and a recipe for mantis mousse.”

My stomach turned once more.

“Enough about insects,” Ardie said. “If Marybeth Potter went off for the weekend, why leave her car behind the tanning place? If she didn’t want to leave it in her garage, or didn’t want to be seen being picked up by the person she went off with, there are plenty of safer places to park.”

"I doubt she was the one who parked it there." I excavated another container. "From what I've heard, she's controlling and cautious."

"From what her daughter told me," Doug said, "she was all about order, neatness, and keeping her possessions safe and in good condition."

"You knew Seleena?"

"Had her as a teaching assistant the year before last." Doug shook his head. "What a waste of time. She couldn't teach a fish how to swim. And as far as assisting was concerned, I would have gotten more help from a loaf of bread. Stale bread."

Teaching assistants were students who had free periods in their schedules. They were assigned to a supervisor and expected to work on their resumes and develop personal and job skills. Several days a week they were farmed out to teachers to help with tasks like making copies, inventorying textbooks, straightening classrooms, and running errands.

"Did you let her supervisor know?" Ardie asked.

"Yes. But he said he was getting the same my-mother-is-on-the-school-board line of intimidation she was handing me. We decided not to press the issue. Life is too short to spend time limping around after you shoot yourself in the foot."

"Good call," Ardie agreed. "Pick your battles. Sometimes it's best to ignore what you can. Try not to engage."

"That's what I did. Or tried to do. I'd suggest she work on assignments for other classes, or research colleges—not that she was on the fast track to higher education, and not that she had much interest in the world beyond the malls in Portland. But she didn't do any of that. When she wasn't comparing shoes with the girls in class or reminding everyone about her mother, she hung around my desk. At first I thought she was just needy, wanting attention. I figured she didn't get much at home. And I'd noticed she didn't have close friends at school."

"Her own fault," Ardie said.

"Yeah. I knew that, but I figured things at home hadn't prepared her to get along well with others. I felt kind of sorry for her. Until the questions started."

"Questions about colleges and teaching programs?" I asked. "About the pros and cons of being a teacher?"

"Sort of." Doug blushed. "But inappropriate questions. Personal questions."

Chapter 15

I waited for him to elaborate, but he said nothing more as he held the trash bag wide for another contribution, this one encased in aluminum foil and sealed with masking tape. A glance at Ardie's face told me she was also impatient.

She cracked first. "How inappropriate? How personal?"

Doug's blush deepened. "I'd rather not say."

"I bet she asked whether you were married," I guessed. "And if not, why not. And if you had a girlfriend. And how much money you made."

"And whether you thought she was too young to date a teacher," Ardie added.

"Pretty much." Doug turned white around the lips. "Made me so nervous I went back through all the training about sexual harassment and other stuff they go over with us at the beginning of the year. I made sure we were never alone. I even went to see Jerome Morrow to go on the record with the administration. But he wasn't in his office and no one knew where he was."

(For the record, Jerome Morrow, the former principal of Captain Meriwether High School, had made a career out of being hard to find. If you've been following my story, you know that's a fact and not a case of speaking ill of the dead.)

"So I told Big Chill the whole story," Doug continued, "and she said she'd let him know and I should put it all in writing. Then she said she'd arrange for Seleena to be transferred to another teacher in a way that wouldn't make it seem like it was my idea."

"And when the Chillster says she'll do something," I said, "it shall be done. And done quickly."

"Yeah. The next day she came up with a song and dance about inventory requirements and put Seleena on a special administrative assignment counting reams of paper and staplers and odds and ends in the business office."

The business office was down a level and on the opposite end of the building from Doug's classroom.

"That must have been a relief."

"A big one."

"But I bet she still hung around," Ardie speculated.

"Right. She'd go out of her way to find me in the halls or waylay me in the parking lot. She'd beg me to tell the Chillster I needed her in my classroom."

"And you told her Big Chill's word was law."

"Pretty much. I was one happy camper when she graduated." He blew out a sigh. "But she's still popping up. Outside the school, at the supermarket, and over here at the rec center. She even cruised by the picket line yesterday."

"Was that her in the pinkish car? Was that why you turned sideways and held your sign in front of your face?"

"Yes. That was her third trip past."

"She's stalking you," Ardie said.

"Yeah. And it's getting worse. She drives by my house. I've seen her several times when I collect my mail. I try to pretend I don't notice her, but that's tough because she honks and waves and even pulls to the curb."

"And you run for cover," Ardie said.

"As fast as I can. It's getting old. Really old."

"Have you thought about getting a restraining order?" Ardie suggested.

"I hate to have to go that far. I mean, she's just a kid."

"A messed up kid," Ardie said.

"Yeah. I was thinking of maybe talking with Dave to see if he had other ideas, but then the contract negotiations broke down."

"And you were worried her mother might leap to her defense and blame you," I finished.

"And take it out on you and every other teacher in the district with a blow to the wallet," Ardie added. "Although it's hard to imagine she could be more set against increasing teacher pay than she was."

"Or is." I scraped sand from another mound. "Or will be when she gets back from . . . wherever."

"Unless whatever happened to her makes for some major opinion changes," Ardie said.

"We can hope." I uncovered another contribution for Doug's trash bag, a bulging plastic container filled with something red and orange.

"Careful," Doug said. "That looks like it's about to burst."

I worked the shovel beneath it and raised it slowly.

"Hold it." Ardie bent to study it. "Can you make out what brand that container is?"

"No," Doug said. "And this is as close as I'm getting."

"Don't ask me to brush off the sand," I added, "because that's not happening. There may not be an antidote for the stuff in there."

"I hadn't thought of that." Ardie straightened and took a step back. "I wanted to get the brand name because I need new containers and I figured that kind would hold up for years. The dogs got it out here without putting a hole in it, so it's got to be sturdy."

"The way the stuff inside is frothing," I said, "it's amazing it hasn't blown the lid off."

"Get out your phone and make a video," Doug ordered Ardie. "The company might buy it to use in their next ad campaign."

I lowered the container into the bag. "What are you thinking of for a slogan?"

"We lock in lethal." He shot me a proud grin.

"Trust us. Your sludge won't budge." I shot him one in return.

"We clamp the top on glop," Ardie contributed.

Laughing, we unearthed the remaining containers. "Forget putting this in your car," Ardie told me. "It's going in Aston's truck with whatever you toss from the refrigerator. He said he was planning to make a dump run soon and he might as well take Brenda's leavings. If he doesn't, I'll tell Tremaine Scott about the day he suggested teaching kids to roll their own cigarettes was an example of living history."

As I've mentioned before, Aston frequently exhibits less common sense than the average moth approaching a flame.

"Is the dump open on Sunday? Or on Labor Day." I asked. "This stuff will be even more toxic if it sits out in this heat until Tuesday."

"Aston won't notice," Doug said. "Have you seen his truck lately?"

"No." I'd ridden in it once by necessity and still sometimes felt the need to stay in the shower an extra minute to scrub away tactile and olfactory memories. I'd vowed to walk, crawl, or slither on my belly rather than accept a ride from him again.

"Is it worse than it was in May?" Ardie asked. "When Tremaine ordered him to park at the far end of the student lot?"

"I didn't get close enough to it then to make an accurate comparison, but I believe it is." Doug waved his hands in a broad circle. "It's a rolling miasma, a stench on wheels, a reek with a gear shift, a—"

"We get it." Ardie held up a hand.

"I'm not sure you do," Doug said with a vicious grin. "But you will when we cart this stuff out to it."

And we did.

Even from several yards away, I could see flies surrounding Aston's truck. The trick, however, would have been not seeing them. There must have been a hundred, and each was the size of a nickel. They lifted and settled and lifted again like dark waves crashing on a rocky shore. Their wings glittered in the sunshine, their buzzing drilled into my eardrums.

And then there was the smell of the cargo in the bed of Aston's truck. It was an amalgamation of odors, a funk stew, a thick and malodorous stench. It was the smell of rot and decay, low tide and burning rubber. It was . . .

Well, let's face it, my language skills aren't extensive enough to create even an adequate description. So I'll abandon the attempt.

Between gags and gasps, Ardie got out a question. "How can he stand to ride in this thing?"

"He probably drives fast. With the windows down," I guessed. "And probably he's smoking one of those cigars he brought to school the day he portrayed Ulysses S. Grant."

"I wish we could toss our sacks and run," Doug said. "But he's already got a mountain of crud in there and I'm afraid if we don't wedge these in they'll tumble right out again."

Great. We were in for an up-close-and-personal encounter.

"Hold your breath as long as you can," Ardie advised. "And breathe through your mouth."

I tried.

It didn't help much.

The stench seemed to be alive. Like a giant amorphous creature, it smacked us down, slimed our skin, seeped into our pores, and zapped the parts of our brains that trigger physical reactions.

I'll leave the nature and extent of those reactions to your imagination and say only that I've had cases of stomach flu that made me feel more like dancing.

Still, while I suffered olfactory overload, my vision remained sharp—or as sharp as vision can be when your eyes water, your glasses need cleaning, and you're overdue for an eye exam you suspect will result in a stronger prescription. But my curiosity wasn't compromised so, as we lugged our trash sacks to the tailgate, hoisted them over, and packed them securely, I scanned what Aston had previously crammed in the bed of the truck. It was a rapid scan, more like a blink, like a camera shutter opening and snapping closed again. But that was enough to create a mental image, enough for me to catalog what I saw as we beat our retreat. A moldy canvas tent, once white but now gray, green, and black. A cane bottom chair with two broken legs and most of the cane in tatters. A rusted frying pan and a collection of bent forks and mangled tin cups and plates, some with what appeared to be claw marks. A box of bones. A box of bits of hide and fur. Two brown leather shoes with square toes, low heels, and small gold buckles. A fish net that appeared to have been made out of grapevine and held at least two small dead fish with sunken and accusing eyes. Several snarls of fishing line. A fringed lampshade. A leaf rake with tines bent in every possible direction.

"Ready for lunch?" Doug asked after we'd stumbled far enough from the truck to draw more than shallow breaths. "I'm buying."

"I'll never eat again," Ardie protested.

I felt the same way.

At least for a few minutes.

But by the time I got home, raced upstairs, shed clothing that had acted as a magnet for the stench, showered, and washed my hair twice, my appetite spiked right back to normal.

(For the record, "normal" for my appetite falls somewhere beyond what a medical professional might call "healthy." To be honest, if there was a hand-over-that-brownie-or-I-won't-be-responsible-for-what-happens-next mark on the appetite scale, I'd hit it daily.)

"Let's see if there's any salad left," I told Cheese Puff.

He shot me a glare that said salad was nothing more than a low-calorie insult, but I scooped him from the nest he'd made among the pillows and carried him downstairs. As I scooted along the hallway bound for the refrigerator, however, my desire for sustenance plummeted. The reason took the form of my sister.

Chapter 16

Iz lounged on one end of the sofa like a warthog wallowing at a muddy waterhole. Not that my sister resembles a warthog. I mean, she couldn't be a stunt double for one. It's more a personality thing. Not that I have firsthand experience with warthog personalities, and not that I want to, but you get the drift.

Cheese Puff lifted his upper lip in a snarl that made his ten-pound body vibrate. I bent to set him on the floor, but he wiggled free before I could release him and streaked back up the stairs. Despite a few moments of grudging acceptance scattered here and there in their history, there's no love lost between my dog and my sister. Occasionally he sticks around to mock her in his own little way, but usually he seeks refuge.

Iz looked up from spearing the final slice of cucumber from the bowl in which I'd stored the leftover salad. "You put way too many olives in this," she said. "And the walnuts were a little soft."

"Thanks for the input," I said in a voice normally reserved for a student discovered writing obscene messages on a whiteboard.

"You're welcome." Iz tossed the fork in the bowl and set it on the sofa before tearing open a bag of corn chips. "You're out of salsa. Except for the really hot kind I don't like."

The fact that Iz didn't like it was a glowing recommendation for the brand I'd purchased. I made a mental note to put it on the list for the next shopping excursion.

Dave, clutching the remote in one hand and his cellphone in the other, shot me a sympathetic wince before snapping his gaze back to the baseball game on TV. I checked the score in the upper corner and saw the Yankees were playing the Orioles and winning. Normally—unless they played the Mariners—the Yankees were on Dave's no-watch list. But if the objective is to avoid conversing with a warthog, a man will resort to desperate measures.

"Couldn't find a tiddlywinks tournament?" I asked him.

"It's on next. I'm killing time until it gets underway."

"And cooling down from your run?"

I tried for a note of innocence, but snarkiness prevailed. Dave was still barefooted and there were no signs he'd already logged a few miles, no running shoes and socks dropped on the floor by the sofa.

"Some days you don't need to run to raise your pulse rate or break out in a sweat." He cut his gaze toward Iz who was eating corn chips in a manner not unlike that of a wood chipper laying waste to a sapling. "Some days, when the people you live with forget to lock the door, you get a workout without leaving the couch."

I mouthed "sorry" and headed for the pantry and the family-size container of oatmeal where I'd stashed a trove of malted milk balls. Normally I eat them one at a time, savoring each one. Not today. I crammed five in my mouth and crunched them down as I replaced the container beside boxes of breakfast cereal. Then I went on the hunt for something with more nutritional value.

(For the record, having had my taste buds set on experiencing the remaining salad—soggy walnuts or not—the hunt wasn't what you'd call a rousing success. Plus, pickings were slim. There was end-of-the-package cheese and turkey to go with end-of-the-package bread. There were two kinds of mustard and mayonnaise of the little-bit-left-in-the-bottle variety. There was lettuce as wilted as a bouffant hairdo in a rainstorm. There were eggs and olives, maple syrup and orange juice, broccoli and pickles. And there were things in containers that I had no desire to examine closely. They reminded me far too much of what Brenda left behind. And that reminded me of Aston's truck.

My appetite retreated like a sunning seal spotting a polar bear.

"When you're finished rooting around," my sister said, "I want to talk to you."

More like talk *at* me.

Certainly not talk *with* me.

"Is it about what you called to tell me yesterday?"

"Yes." Iz shot a double-barreled glare at Dave. "I can't make him see that my project—our project—should take precedence over everything else." She smacked a pristine legal pad on the sofa between them. "I came over to brainstorm."

I shuddered. Thinking about what went on in my sister's brain was scary enough without imagining a storm raging among the synapses.

"This is vital." She smacked the pad again. "Nothing else is as important. Nothing."

As if on cue, Dave's cellphone buzzed. He raised it to his face so fast I thought he'd break his nose. As he read the text he got an expression of relief and deliverance like I hadn't seen since I offered to do the vacuuming if he brought home dinner. "Duty calls. There's crime to fight. Wrong to right."

Really?

"Too bad your superhero suit is in the wash."

"Suits are for sissies." He clicked off the TV, leaped to his feet, and headed for the stairs. "You two have a nice chat."

I wanted to taunt him right back, but nothing leaped to my mind or lips. I made an attempt to satisfy my curiosity instead. "Is it about Marybeth Potter?"

"You know I can't tell you about on-going cases."

You just did, I thought. But I kept my lips zipped so as not to tip him to the fact that he'd hesitated a bit too long before answering my question.

"See," Iz fumed. "The least little thing and he races off. Everything else is more important than my project."

"*Your* project?"

She scowled. "Well, technically, like I said before, it's our project, but obviously I'm putting far more effort into getting it off the ground than he is."

And she was—but only if by effort she meant flailing around, and only if a millimeter above the earth counted as being off the ground. "Maybe you should consider starting small and hunting for local money."

Iz swelled out her chest, making the image of the goddess of victory on the front of her T-shirt spread her wings wider. "I am not the kind of person who starts small."

This was true.

In more ways than one.

Iz at birth had weighed close to 11 pounds. That's as hefty as a medium-size watermelon. To further put it in context, she weighed more than Cheese Puff. Legend had it my mother had cried for a week and been unable to sit down for two. Why she had another child—namely me—was something I couldn't understand. But, having given birth to exactly zero children of my own, I expected there was a lot about biological drives and maternal instincts I also didn't get.

Dressed in jeans and a sheriff's department T-shirt, and carrying a pair of leather boots, two pairs of socks, a flannel shirt, a ball cap, and a windbreaker, Dave hurtled down the stairs. He flipped me a wave and headed for the door. "Don't wait up."

Hmmm.

That comment and his attire told me two other things about his mission. There was no set time for it to conclude, and it would take place in rough terrain.

The logical conclusion was he'd been called to join in a search.

And unless someone else was missing, the search was for Marybeth Potter.

I'd tuned Iz out while I formed my hypothesis. Now I tuned her back in.

"I have a national reputation," she said with conviction.

A fast-fading reputation. Except for a local foray or two, she'd been off the conference speaker/rabble rouser circuit for a couple of years. The public had moved on.

"The national arena is where the vision is," she continued. "I refuse to demean myself by pandering to tight-fisted tiny organizations for a few nickels and dimes. I will not . . ."

I tuned her out once more and put my mind to considering how I could find out where Dave was searching and whether he was looking for articles of clothing, the contents of a purse, signs of a struggle, or a body. None of Dave's colleagues would give me more than the time of day—if that. The only possible way of finding out would be to call Stan Stewart and ask for repayment for all the tips I'd provided. Knowing him, he'd make me grovel. Unless there was chocolate involved, I hated to grovel.

"You haven't heard a word I said," my sister thundered. "I might as well talk to your ridiculous little dog."

I didn't refute that because, seriously, it was pretty darn accurate.

"You can't even bother to try to defend yourself, can you?" Iz stood, brushed corn chips crumbs from her cargo shorts onto the coffee table and sofa, and picked up her still-blank legal pad. "I'm going where I'm appreciated."

There were few places that met the appreciation criteria, but the main one was the home she shared with her partner Penelope. To get a mental picture of her, think of the saying about opposites attracting.

"Say hello to Penelope for me," I said in a cheery voice. "Tell her I'm looking forward to seeing her soon, like the next time Mrs. B arranges a barbecue on the deck."

Iz rubbed her stomach. "When's that?"

"Don't know." And that was the beauty of it. With gobs of money at her command and catering companies on speed dial, Mrs. B could toss together dinner al fresco whenever the whim struck.

Iz stopped rubbing and squinted. Let me assure you that her scrunched up face was not a pretty sight. "You sure you don't know? You sure you wouldn't 'accidentally' forget to tell me?"

"Never."

Well, at least I wouldn't forget to tell her accidentally.

"Hrmph." Iz tromped toward the door.

I followed, intending to lock it after she departed and thus prevent the only thing worse than a visit from my sister—a second visit minutes later.

The only thing worse than a second visit from Iz was an encounter with the person standing on the doorstep with a raised fist.

Chapter 17

Bernina Burke, the woman who called herself our condo manager but couldn't manage to find feathers in a chicken coop, never knocked when she could hammer with her fist. And she usually embellished the hammering with a few kicks.

Iz and Bernina had history—history along the lines of France and England in the 1700s, or the U.S. and Russia since World War II. In other words, they weren't BFFs.

"You," Iz said in a voice stuffed with scorn.

"You," Bernina uttered with deep disgust.

"Out of my way."

Iz stepped into Bernina's personal space.

"Or what?"

Bernina, once squarely in my sister's weight class, had been shedding pounds at a slow but steady rate. She was still in the same personality and attitude class though, so she didn't give an inch.

I, however, scuttled crablike toward the living room to avoid becoming collateral damage when they clashed.

"Or what?" Bernina asked from between gritted teeth.

My sister unsnapped a bulging pocket above her right knee and reached inside.

I reversed, scuttled closer, and craned my neck. Since the day Iz patted a pocket and said she could handle a tough situation because she was packing, Dave and I had often speculated about the nature of her weaponry.

"Or what?" Bernina repeated.

Iz withdrew a black canister, and aimed the nozzle at her nemesis. "Or this."

Was that pepper spray?

I craned my neck another few millimeters but, if the canister had a label, my sister's hand obscured it.

"You wouldn't dare," Bernina hissed.

"Don't be so sure." Iz tapped her forefinger on the button at the top of the canister.

I scuttled along the hallway once again. If Iz made good on her threat, the stuff might drift. Or, worse, Bernina might be temporarily blinded and enraged beyond reason. She might charge into the condo and smash into me. I might be flattened like a cartoon character. I might wind up with permanent footprints on my face.

"Oh, I'm sure all right," Bernina snarled. "I'm sure you're certifiable. And I'm sure that, unlike some people, I have meaningful and vital business to attend to this afternoon. I can't afford to be sidetracked by someone who can't find a real job and spends her time running around making trouble."

She stepped back and to one side, bowing and motioning with one arm as if to usher Iz from the condo.

I expected immediate verbal fireworks and possible physical assault, but my sister hesitated, saying nothing, her finger tapping the button. Then she returned the canister to her pocket and fastened the snap. "I can't afford to waste my time either."

Bernina scowled but, to my surprise, said nothing.

Iz took her leave, treading close to the toes of Bernina's orange tennis shoes. Meanwhile, I decided this confrontation had ended in a tie. Licking my right index finger, I made two marks in the air on my imaginary scoreboard, one mark to the right and one to the left.

"What's that about?" Bernina asked as, uninvited, she strode down the hallway. Her XL yellow shirt flapped and billowed and her corduroy shorts—created by hacking a pair of slacks off at the knees—whiffled as she walked.

Clearly someone needed to record this for a sound-effects library. Clearly another someone should perform a wardrobe intervention.

But that someone wasn't me.

"Nothing." I retreated to the far side of the dining room and licked my finger again. "Cut myself shaving."

Bernina didn't ask further questions, but cut to the chase. "If you'd read the condo association rules, you'd know we don't allow yard sales on the premises."

"Huh? I'm not having a yard sale."

Bernina pointed to Mrs. B's unit. "Your neighbor is."

"Mrs. Ballantine? What gives you that idea?"

"Her car is full of junk."

Ah.

Bernina had spotted the stuff Mrs. B salvaged from Verna's storage locker.

No way would I clue her about the origin of said stuff. Verna's place had been a fire hazard before we cleaned it out. But Verna had been such a private—or should I say secretive?—person none of us knew of the danger. And there was no reason for Bernina to learn about it now. She was liable to cite some arcane and possibly nonexistent condo regulation. She might demand to inspect Verna's place, upsetting my neighbor and perhaps causing a medical setback.

The only thing to do was go on the offensive. "So what? I haven't seen her car, but having a few odds and ends in the back seat doesn't mean she's planning a yard sale. Maybe she's redecorating."

"With junk? That's not her style."

Good point. "Maybe she's helping a friend move."

"Where? To the city dump?" Bernina's gaze strafed my living room. "*Most* of her friends have better taste. They wouldn't possess any of the crap I saw in her car."

The implication was I was the exception, the friend who would happily strew the contents of her car about my abode. The implication was I had less taste than a pack rat.

I scraped the recesses of my mind for a comeback and got nothing. So I fell back on what was tried and true. "So what? You set the bar for good taste now? Hah! Your outfit isn't exactly fit for a runway, unless it's an airport runway. And I'm surprised the health department hasn't cited your car as a sanitation hazard."

In fact, I actually wouldn't have been surprised. Bernina's car is a rolling trash can, a place where burger wrappers and diet soda cans lingered for months, a place where the seeds in an apple core might sprout in a drift of used napkins, junk mail, advertising flyers, and paper bags.

She folded her arms, arms still meaty. "So?"

"So I don't barge into your office and accuse you of planning to violate condo rules. I don't insult your choices in furniture and accessories."

Mirroring her, I folded my arms as well. And okay, they weren't exactly smoothly muscled. And, okay again, there were what you might call wings of flab on their undersides. But only short and stubby wings.

"Besides, why are you here? Why are you harping at me? If you have a problem with Mrs. Ballantine, go talk with her."

Bernina frowned and I chortled inwardly. No way would she go next door. First, like many of us, she had a healthy respect for Mrs. B, a respect that often crept along the scale to trepidation and even outright fear. Second, Mrs. B, although as frustrated with Bernina as the rest of us, had been comparatively kind to her. Once she'd even engineered a hair and makeup makeover and paid for wardrobe upgrades that, based on Bernina's outfit today, were due for serious revisiting and renewal. And third, although Mrs. B made every effort to keep it a secret, I was willing to bet Cheese Puff's dental bling that Bernina had heard of the move my neighbor was spearheading to change condo rules.

The change would eliminate a paid manager in favor of a committee of residents who would be compensated for their time and effort through discounts on their monthly fees. Older condo residents living on fixed incomes were fully onboard with the concept because it would save them money. Others were all for it because it would save them from Bernina Burke.

Bernina had a contract with plenty of time remaining, but Mrs. B believed shoddy record-keeping and the fact that she'd toyed with the idea of trying to increase the condo emergency fund by playing the slot machines, might be more than enough to void the contract. I tended to agree, especially because when Mrs. B crooked her little finger the biggest legal gun in the county came out of retirement and stood ready to do her bidding.

Until she was fully prepared and ready to take action, Mrs. B quietly studied Bernina's official job description, read and reread condo rules, lobbied residents, and counted potential votes. Bernina, meanwhile, continued to fill out applications for management positions at other condo complexes, chasing her dream of running a larger place, making more money, and terrorizing a greater number of residents.

In the interest of helping her achieve that goal, many of the rest of us practiced the art of lying when questioned by residents of other condo complexes. Jim had even compiled a list of possible responses and passed along copies. It included short sentences that those of us who knew Bernina found to be only half true, but others might accept as valid and complete.

To clarify, I'll note a few, providing the missing information in parentheses. She has a straightforward approach (like a tank crossing open ground). She's done a lot to get residents working as a community (against her). She has years of experience (annoying residents). If she leaves she'll be missed (the same way a headache is after it's gone). We always listen when she speaks (because she's so loud it's hard not to).

"Go on," I repeated. "Go talk to Mrs. B."

Bernina's frown softened to what I'd guess was an expression of serious contemplation—if she was the kind of person who ever did such a thing, or knew how. I turned aside and began sorting through the growing stack of menus, ads, and bills wedged beneath the phone at the edge of the kitchen counter. No way would I contribute unnecessary syllables, phrases, or even clauses that might prolong this conversation. If indeed that's what this could be called.

Bernina sighed, letting out what felt like sufficient air to inflate enough balloons to bend and twist into a herd of balloon animals. "Well, if you're sure she's not planning a yard sale, I guess I'll be off. I was just doing my job."

By employing all the willpower in my arsenal, I forced myself to sustain a neutral expression. Nodding, I concentrated on a newspaper insert advertising cilantro soap.

"Just doing what a condo manager is supposed to do," Bernina added in a cheery voice. "You know, being proactive, taking care of little problems before they become big ones, always considering the greater good of the majority of the residents here at 90 Columbia Lane."

Biting my lip, I read more about cilantro soap. Since I was one of those who couldn't eat the green leafy stuff without tasting soap, I decided putting cilantro *in* soap was a stroke of genius. That way, I knew right where it was. That way I wouldn't accidentally get a mouthful of it blended into salad dressings or chopped so fine in a casserole that I couldn't spot it without the use of a microscope.

"So, I'll be running along," Bernina babbled. "Be sure to call me if you have any concerns."

Concerns?

Like almost every adult on the planet, I had a whole slew of major concerns—concerns about pollution and rising taxes, healthcare and education, global warming and comets on collision courses with earth. And then there were minor concerns—like why manufacturers discontinue a product or flavor the minute I decide it's my favorite, why the number of hot dogs snug in their package doesn't match the number of buns nestled in their plastic sack, why I always have a bad-hair day when I need to look my best, and why I never get a zit when I've planned to spend the day at home.

Then there was the question of what happened to Marybeth Potter.

But Bernina clearly meant concerns about the condo complex. And I had a whole slew of those as well. I had concerns about her lack of financial skills, her lack of ability to retain maintenance and landscaping companies, and her tendency to leap to erroneous conclusions. But bringing any of that up would cause her to linger, so I only nodded and used the newspaper insert to wave goodbye.

Three seconds after I'd locked the door, I snatched up the phone and dialed Mrs. B. "Bernina was just here asking me whether you intend to have a yard sale with the junk in your car. When I insisted you weren't planning to violate condo rules, she claimed to believe me. And, get this, she said she was sorry to bother me."

"Really?"

"Really. And she backed away from a fight with Iz."

"Really?"

"Really."

"Well, those are certainly departures from her usual behavior."

"Major departures. I think she knows what you're up to."

"And she's changing her attitude to try to head me off," Mrs. B mused.

"But you won't be headed off, will you?" I asked in a hopeful voice.

Chapter 18

Mrs. B didn't answer right away.

I groaned.

"Now, dear," Mrs. B said in a voice so flat and rational it could have issued from a robot. "You know I have a lot on my plate. If Bernina has seen the error of her ways and becomes a better manager, we can let things ride until her contract expires. That way there's no need to waste hours of my time. And no need for Angus to prepare to litigate."

"Even if Bernina had a personality transplant," I seethed, "she'd be back to her old ways before the incision healed."

"Now, dear, I'm sure that's an exaggeration."

But not much of one.

"Perhaps Bernina has realized it's in her best interests to change."

Perhaps polar bears will decide they'd look better in basic black.

"She could be approaching a milestone in her career."

If making everyone miserable could be considered a career.

"Have you noticed there's a difference of only one letter between milestone and millstone?"

Mrs. B said nothing. From past experience I knew that was her polite way of indicating she wasn't about to extend the discussion/argument. But, since I'm not as highly evolved, I felt free to slip in another comment before I disconnected. “If she makes enough progress for you to drop your campaign to oust her, we’ll have her around our necks until we drown in an ocean of incompetence.”

I took a breath and finished up. “Incompetence without an ounce of etiquette or fashion sense.”

Then, like a spiteful child, I disconnected.

I barely got the phone back in its cradle when it rang.

“Not answering,” I crowed at it, confident the caller was Mrs. B. “Not giving you even half a chance to convince me I’m exaggerating.”

The phone rang once more, the readout displaying a number I hadn’t seen before. I let it ring one more time before curiosity got the better of me. I picked it up, clicked it on, and held it to my ear without saying a word.

“Gotta make this quick,” Stan Stewart said. “I’m on a borrowed phone because I don’t want to miss a call I’m expecting on mine. Tell me what you know.”

“I know I’m hungry.” I carried the phone to the pantry in the fond hope I might have overlooked a sack of cookies. Or perhaps the can of chili had morphed into a slab of banana cream pie.

“What do you know about the Potter case?”

“Nothing I didn’t read in the paper.”

“You sure?”

“Positive.”

I moved the can of chili, peered behind it, and remembered Dave taking off like a weasel freed from a trap. “Except I know that Dave got called in.”

“When?”

“Half an hour ago maybe.”

"Did he tell you anything?"

"Not to wait up."

"That's all."

"Yes."

Stewart uttered several expletives best left deleted.

"He took along a pair of leather boots," I offered. "And a flannel shirt. And a windbreaker. I think he expected to be in rough terrain and probably out late."

"I knew you knew more," Stewart chortled.

I hate when he does that. It makes me want to hit him with a flyswatter the size of a beach towel. "So that qualifies you as a genius? How about telling me what you know? And don't give me any guff about protecting your sources."

"Right now I wish I had sources. Or at least sources that knew something and would give it up. I'm hearing a lot of chatter on the scanner. Can't pick up anything definite, but I think they found something. Maybe her purse."

"Where?"

"Don't know yet. Uh, gotta go."

And that was it. No mention of thanks or intention to call me later. In short, the experience reminded me of some of my college dating experiences.

I replaced the phone, replaced the can of chili, and reviewed my dining options. Nothing appetizing. I'd find plenty of tasty options next door, but I'd just been snarky to Mrs. B, so I'd have to crawl on my belly to get at them.

On the positive side, I had only myself to consider because Allison was out with Josh and Dave was out on what smart money said was a search. I had a stack of takeout menus, a couple of fresh mysteries from the library, and no chores drastically in need of immediate attention. Outside, a light breeze was blowing, the afternoon was cooling down nicely, and I had a new lounge chair with puffy cushions I'd picked up at an end-of-summer sale.

Decision made, I headed upstairs to get a sun hat and my entitled little dog.

Allison returned a few seconds before her curfew, but Dave still wasn't home when the alarm sounded a few minutes before 6:00 Monday morning. I splashed water on my face and hustled downstairs where I snapped on the radio just in time to hear the music that signaled the start of Jake's show. The musical selections varied according to his mood and had been written and recorded by a guy who, amazingly, owed my ex money instead of the other way around. Jake had about a dozen selections—all reminiscent of what I think of as ego-heavy tunes about doing things my way, having someone under my thumb, or being too sexy for whatever.

And then Jake was on the air, informing his listeners that although many of them had the day off, he was on the job. And not only that, but he was about to bring them a very special show including the first installment of a new regular feature called "Let's Bake with Jake."

I could almost hear Deming gagging.

"It all starts in 90 minutes," Jake announced, "so brew up the coffee and get ready to measure and mix along with me and a woman on the cutting edge of culinary . . . culinary . . . cooking." He whooped the final word as if it was exactly the one he'd intended to use all along.

I bet myself that Deming was also dizzy and sweating. Listening to Jake work without a script was a lot like riding with a novice driver. On a Los Angeles freeway. During rush hour. In a car without brakes or a steering wheel.

Chuckling, I snapped off the radio and headed upstairs to shower. Killing time, I plucked my eyebrows, shaved my legs, and applied fresh sparkly silver polish to my toenails, noting as I did that the bottle I'd purchased two weeks ago was half empty. To make it tougher for Allison to find and appropriate, I hid the tiny container at the bottom of the dirty clothes hamper.

At 7:00 I skipped downstairs, retrieved the morning paper, and brewed a pot of coffee. Stan Stewart's short article on the front page confirmed that a purse believed to belong to Marybeth Potter had been discovered near a county park famous for waterfalls and swimming holes. The way he indicated a search was underway without actually saying that made me suspect the police were releasing darn little in the way of official information. I powered up my laptop, checked Portland news outlets, and found nothing more.

I pulled the pot from the coffeemaker and stuck a mug under the stream of dark brew, capturing enough to get my brain in gear, and adding a slug of milk to cool it. Sipping, I thought about Marybeth Potter and the county park. It was short on facilities and several miles from a main highway along a twisting county road. Like too many county roads, that one was in need of widening and resurfacing and was crowded on both sides by enormous blackberry hedges. Their canes had raked the sides of my car when I'd driven Allison to the park earlier in the summer to meet up with friends. As I drove, I'd wondered if I'd blow out a tire or break an axle. Trying to avoid potholes and cracks in the pavement was like trying to avoid paying taxes or growing older.

I'd seen almost no homes along the way, and those I spotted appeared to be abandoned or sadly in need of major repair. Their yards were overgrown and littered with broken swing sets and abandoned vehicles sinking into the landscape like prehistoric animals caught in a tar pit. Even with a maximum of sprucing up, I doubted Marybeth Potter would be the least bit interested in representing any of them.

In short, the area was perfect as a dumping ground for her purse.

And possibly a dumping ground for her body.

The thought of being dumped in the woods in a remote area gave me the shivers. Fortunately, it was time to switch on the radio for what I had no doubt would be comic relief. Not, I guessed, for Deming Featherstone and Dario O'Brien. But I bet the bulk of the Reckless River radio audience was in for a few laughs.

"You can't see me," Jake said, "but I'm walking down the hall from my studio to the radio station's kitchen where Brenda Waring, a chef renowned for many unique and interesting dishes using locally sourced eels as the prime ingredient, is preparing to make . . . preparing to cook . . . Well, uh, Brenda, why don't you tell everyone what you're creating for us?"

Brenda's answer, when it finally came, consisted of one word delivered in a high-pitched and quavering voice. "Eggs."

In the dead air that followed, I could almost hear Deming chortling.

"What kind of eggs?" Jake asked.

"Benedict," Brenda whispered.

Out of curiosity, I brought my laptop to life and searched for recipes to see exactly how complicated this would be. Except for tempering the egg mixture so you got a sauce instead of lumps of cooked eggs it didn't seem too difficult.

And, in a real kitchen, it probably wouldn't be.

Chapter 19

"Good," Jake said. "Eggs Benedict. Sounds great."

"I'm using smoked eels," Brenda added. "Instead of bacon or ham."

"Terrific," Jake enthused. "Tell us more."

"About what?"

"The eels. They're kind of your thing, right? But eels live in water, don't they?"

At least three seconds passed before Brenda said, "Yes."

"So," Jake said with a chuckle, "isn't it hard to get them lit?"

Another three seconds passed.

"Get it?" Jake asked.

"No," Brenda said.

"Okay, see, I was making a joke. I was, uh, pretending I thought you smoked eels like cigarettes."

"Why would you do that?" Brenda's voice was as flat and hard as the bottom of a cast-iron frying pan. "Eels are nothing like cigarettes."

"Um, yeah. I know that. See, I was preten— Never mind. Tell us about this guy Benedict. Who is he?"

"The one who came up with the recipe?" Brenda guessed.

"Does he live here in Reckless River?"

"Uh, um, possibly."

"Ha!" I pounded the table hard enough to slosh coffee. According to the information that came up along with the recipe, Lemuel Benedict, often credited with creating the dish, died around 1943. Unless he came back to life and moved across the continent, he wasn't a Reckless River resident.

To my total lack of surprise, neither Jake nor Brenda had done a lick of research.

"Do you think he might be listening this morning?" Jake asked.

"Er, uh, maybe."

"If he is, I hope he'll give us a call and let us know what he thinks about using eels."

I slapped the table again, partly with glee and partly because of the pain I felt for Deming. This segment was falling apart even faster than I'd anticipated.

"Well, let's get started," Jake prompted. "I'll help. What do we do first?"

"Separate the eggs."

"Great. I'll put one on the table and one in the refrigerator and one on top of—"

"Not that way." Brenda's voice grew louder and sharper, much the way it sounded when she was annoyed at Aston.

"Oh," Jake said. "Oh, I see what you're doing. Let me get the microphone real close and try to do one myself."

I guessed that Op must have increased the volume because the resulting crack sounded like a window shattering.

"And now I kind of juggle the halves of the shells like you're doing," Jake said. "Boy, this is tough while I'm holding the microphone and this clear stuff is slimy. It's dripping everywhere. It's all over my hands and—oops. The yellow part just fell on the floor. If I pick it up before five seconds we can still use it, right?"

"No."

"You sure? Because I thought I heard—"

"No," Brenda repeated. "Step away from the eggs."

"Okay." There was a clatter of sound followed by a rubbing and crumpling I guess was Jake cleaning up with a paper towel. "I'm ready for the next job."

"There is no next job for you." Brenda's voice cracked like a whip. "Stand over there out of my way."

"But you have to give me something else to do," Jake whined. "I promised my listeners I would help."

Brenda's sigh sounded like a spawning tornado. "Fine. You can toast the English muffins while I melt butter for the sauce. There's a toaster over by the refrigerator."

"Great. If you've just tuned in," Jake said in an upbeat voice, "I'm with cooking instructor Brenda Waring and we're about to make some world-class eggs, uh, eggs Ben, uh, eggs Dick, uh, well, eggs something. I'm going to toast muffins now. Not muffins like blueberry, but the English kind."

I heard the sound of shuffling, plastic crinkling, and then a series of grunts. "They won't fit in the toaster."

"You have to split them in half." Brenda's tone was as corrosive as battery acid.

In a moment she added, "No. Not in half that way. You want two rounds, not two half moons."

"That's why we have an expert with us, folks," Jake blathered. "To share important cooking tips like that one. Now I'll just push this lever down and find out what we'll be doing next. I see Brenda has two hot plates plugged in.

She's melting butter in a pan on one of them and on the other is a pot filled with water. I wonder what that's for."

"Poaching the eggs. Is it simmering yet?"

"Simmering," Jake repeated. "That must be a technical cooking term. Can you tell my listeners what it means?"

"A simmer is just below a boil. It's almost there."

"That's amazing. You can tell just be looking? Don't you have to use a thermometer or stick your finger in the—?"

"No," Brenda screamed.

A prolonged howl came next.

It was followed by a splash, a sizzle, a crash, another howl, an electronic sputter, and a series of whimpers.

And then Deming's voice broke in. "Due to technical difficulties, we will not be able to broadcast the remainder of today's episode of 'Let's Bake with Jake.' And now a word from one of our sponsors."

A woman with as much musical talent as a rusty hinge launched into a zippy little tune promoting the benefits of trusting your next colonoscopy to the most qualified folks, the ones with the latest equipment for checking out your equipment, the ones who really knew one end of the business from the other. The commercial was so bad it was good—in a campy kind of way. I knew Dario was one heck of a salesman, but getting a clinic to advertise this procedure with a song was epic.

The jingle ended and Deming returned, his voice riding the edge of what I suspected was hysterical laughter. "My apologies to our listeners. Due to an unfortunate occurrence, Jake Stranahan will be unable to continue today's show. He will return tomorrow. In the meantime, I'm Deming Featherstone and this morning we're talking about the teachers' strike here in Reckless River and the disappearance of a member of the school board. If you have thoughts or comments or questions, the number to call—"

I snapped off the radio, my mind swirling with questions. Not questions about Marybeth Potter or the strike, but about Jake and Brenda. I had no doubt that Jake had burned himself and I could make a rough guess about how that had played out. First he stuck his hand in the pot of hot water, and then he upset the pot when he jerked away from the heat. That sent a cascade of hot water down his pants and shorted out a connection to his microphone. As he danced with pain, he grabbed for the counter in an attempt to keep his balance and touched the hot plate or perhaps brought down the pan of melting butter. Then, in even more serious pain, he'd collapsed on the floor, probably assuming the fetal position.

And now?

Were they on the way to an urgent care center? Would Jake's love life be put on hold while certain vital parts of his male anatomy healed? Would Brenda ask for a return engagement? Would Deming reconsider his career options? Would Dario cancel Jake's contract? Would Dario fire me for advising Deming to stand aside and let the train wreck happen?

While I was considering the positive side of that—free Saturday mornings once more—the landline rang, and Ardie's name came up in the display. I snatched the receiver. "What's up? Are we picketing today?"

"No, but if you can tear yourself away from the ruination on the radio there's an informal meeting of all teachers in the district at 10:00."

Ugh.

Have I mentioned that I hate meetings? Especially meetings promising to be long, drawn-out, and most likely inconclusive?

"And I'm invited?" I asked, trying not to tip her that I hoped the answer would be negative.

"Not technically. Neither am I, but I'm going."

As a sub, I wasn't a member of the teachers' union. As an educational assistant, Ardie belonged to a different union.

"How the teachers' bargaining goes could influence our negotiations," she said. "If anyone objects to either of us being there, we'll leave. Until then we'll hang in the back."

"The back of where?"

"The downtown theater. The owner offered us the space as long as we're out before the first showing at noon."

The downtown theater was high on my list of favorite places. A throwback to Reckless River's earlier days, it was a little art deco, a little retro, and a little frayed around the edges. But it offered candy bars, cold beer, and fresh popcorn at reasonable prices. Just the thought of the snack bar created a puddle of drool beneath my tongue.

I swallowed. "Will the concession stand be open?"

Ardie let out a heartless little laugh and disconnected.

Chapter 20

Taking that to mean the only popcorn on hand would be in kernel form and stored in a cabinet, I set about making breakfast to sustain myself. Pickings were slim because, as you know, my sister had descended on us, and also because Dave and I had been playing a game of chicken with the grocery shopping. The bread selection was paltry—two bits of crust from a loaf of whole wheat and a slice of rye dry enough to qualify as a large crouton. Only one egg remained in the carton and the sell-by date was last week. The milk, what there was of it, was okay. There was a thick smear of butter stuck to the lid of its container and a quarter inch of syrup in the bottle. I spread the smear and poured the syrup on a grim little buckwheat pancake. It was from at least a month ago and had remained uneaten by lurking behind the plastic tub designed to catch cubes spewed by the ice maker.

Nuking the pancake didn't do much for its texture, and the resulting aroma reminded me a little of the contents of Aston's truck. I rolled it up and ate it, chewing as fast as I could while mentally reeling off the benefits of buckwheat.

(For the record, I know there are hordes of people who love the taste. And I know buckwheat has lots of fiber and antioxidants and can help lower cholesterol and blood pressure. And I know those things can contribute to better health and a longer life. But at the moment, all I could do was wonder whether I could fully enjoy a longer life that involved a daily diet of buckwheat pancakes on a par with this one.)

I left a note for Allison indicating we had a supply of OJ and those jam-filled pastries she stuck in the toaster and occasionally remembered to remove before the jam melted out and burned. Then I hiked back to the bedroom, pried Cheese Puff from Dave's pillow—a spot he feels entitled to but is smart enough not to claim when Dave is in residence—and carried him out to the deck.

Like royalty in a sedan chair, he surveyed his domain from my arms. Sunlight flashed from the windshields of cars crossing the bridge to Portland and sparkled on small ripples on the Columbia. The river seemed placid, but I knew from past experience—namely the two times I'd nearly drowned in it—that the current was powerful. And tenacious.

Cheese Puff turned his head, scanning the trail that ran between the condo complex landscaping and a low stone wall atop the riverbank. I suspected he was searching for the rogue duck that had bested him in a one-sided battle last year. And when he rubbed his head against my shoulder I was certain. "Apricot drove the duck off, remember? She saved your little orange butt."

He lifted his upper lip in disdain as if to say he hadn't needed the help of the half-grown cat from the unit beyond Mrs. B's and could have triumphed over the duck in the second round. I chuckled and lowered him to the deck. "Dream on. You would have needed even more stitches if you'd stayed in the ring."

Head held high to make it clear he was snubbing me, he trotted to the far side of the large deck Mrs. B and I had shared since she helped me buy the condo next to hers and removed the privacy panel. I followed and unlatched the gate, allowing him to descend the short flight of wooden steps to the tiny rose garden and the bark mulch spread liberally among the plants.

Normally, he bounced down those steps without a problem. But not today. If you recall the old adage about pride going before a fall, then you can guess what happened next.

Yes, he fell.

He sprawled.

He tumbled.

He reached the bottom and performed a face plant.

Had this been an Olympic event, he would have wiped the floor with the competition. He would have returned home dragging a gold medal larger than his head.

As it was, after relieving himself, he dragged his scruffy body up the steps and limped toward the door at the speed of the last tablespoon of cold catsup emerging from a slightly tilted bottle.

I caught the performance from the corner of my eye. Staring would, I knew, lead to laughing. A lot of laughing. And laughter would lead to a further wounding of his pride. That could result in weeks of payback.

"What happened?" Mrs. B hustled toward us, teal-colored ostrich feathers on her high-heeled bedroom slippers fluttering, heels striking the deck like hailstones. "Did my darling little guy break his leg?"

Before I could say I thought it was only a sprain, she scooped him up, brushed bark bits from his hair, and kissed his knobby little head. "Was he attacked?"

Cheese Puff, I swear, looked at me and nodded as if encouraging me to go with that story and guarantee maximum sympathy. I gave him the tried-and-true substitute teacher scowl. "He had his head up in snub mode and he fell down the steps."

Mrs. B narrowed her eyes as if to say she suspected there was more to the story. "Of course you'll take him to the emergency clinic immediately."

"Um, well, the fall was really more of a tumble, so I thought I'd watch him for—"

"But time is of the essence when it comes to serious injury."

"I know, but I don't think this—"

She raised her right hand in an imperious manner. "You are not a veterinarian, are you?"

Cheese Puff turned his beady little eyes my way. His expression made it clear he enjoyed seeing me put in my place.

"Let's not quibble, dear." Mrs. B lowered her hand and patted my arm. "I know I tend to overreact where the little darling is concerned. And I'm well aware that the emergency clinic can be expensive, especially since he'll probably require an X-ray and perhaps even a cast."

I smothered a smile at visions of Mrs. B insisting we all sign the cast, Mrs. B shopping for a miniature wheelchair, and Mrs. B calling physical therapists in search of one with canine experience.

"So I'll be happy to take him and see to his needs."

And probably take him by a pet supply store later for the latest in designer dog treats. Or a new collar. After all, the one he had on—blue leather with silver stars—was more than two weeks old.

Cheese Puff shot me a glare that clearly told me I was a pathetic excuse for a companion human. I did a mental eye roll and glanced at my watch. "Thank you," I told Mrs. B in the humblest voice I could muster without bringing up my breakfast. "I promised Ardie I'd meet her downtown. The teachers are gathering to—"

"And you need to be there, dear, demonstrating solidarity with your friends." She patted my arm once more. "Dario will drive us as soon as he emerges from the shower and has his coffee."

That told me Dario hadn't listened to Jake's show. If he had, he'd be racing to the radio station. Or to the hospital. I kept my lips zipped. Who was I to upset their Labor Day plans?

"After he's seen the doctor, I'll take him along with us to the park for the Labor Day celebration. Several political newcomers will be speaking and Cheese Puff is an excellent judge of character. I have no doubt he'll let me know which ones I should support."

I swallowed a few choice comments about a dartboard or a crystal ball being more effective than my dog at determining which candidates would receive hefty donations from her bank account. And, much as I'm sure you want to know, I didn't ask how Cheese Puff indicated his choices. I suspected the question would be viewed not only as sarcastic, but also as proof that I didn't believe my little mutt was anywhere as intelligent as Mrs. B did.

And the fact of the matter was that I didn't.

Oh, I readily admitted he was smart, clever, cunning, sneaky, cagey, sly, and opportunistic. And I admitted he understood a great deal of what was said. But could he listen to a political stump speech and sift through the catch phrases and dog whistles and finger-pointing? Could he separate false promises from what was possible? Could he overlay their agendas on Mrs. B's and see which aligned most closely?

I kind of doubted it.

But I all I said was, "I'm sure he'll enjoy the event and I know he'll recover quickly just by being with you."

Cheese Puff yipped agreement.

Mrs. B twinkled a smug smile.

I left for the theater.

Even though I was 15 minutes early, every parking space on streets near the theater was already taken. Some vehicles, bearing pro-education signs taped to the windows, clearly belonged to teachers. I spotted Gertrude's little electric model. A block away, outside a quiche shop, its tires over the line that designated a loading zone, I found Aston's truck. To my total lack of surprise, it still bore its dump-bound load. I doubted the shop owner would be thrilled when she arrived to set out sidewalk tables for the lunch trade. I imagined she'd call the police. And perhaps the health department as well.

Cruising in a widening spiral, I spotted a head-in parking space near the tiny jewelry store that Dave and I once laughingly referred to as Mrs. B's second home. A firm believer in the power of pearls, she had enough necklaces, rings, and bracelets to outfit a good portion of those invited to a royal wedding. And then there were her diamonds, rubies, and other precious gems. Until a few months ago, she'd been a steady customer at the shop. But then Dario had presented her with a blue pearl pendant. Now it was the only one she wore. Of course, she still slipped on several rings each morning, and still replaced them as she changed outfits for the day's events, but her necklaces languished in a jewelry box the size of the kind of suitcase I'd require for a trip around the world.

As I got out, I noticed a discreet sign in the window announcing a limited-time-only sale. I bet myself the owner, a charming man with the knack of fawning over customers without seeming overly unctuous, was hoping Mrs. B would return to her acquisitive ways. I wondered how long he could hold out before his business became a casualty of malls, chain stores, changing times, ebbing fads, and the vagaries of the economy.

A glance at my watch indicated I had five minutes, so I trotted to the theater on a direct route instead of one that wouldn't take me past Aston's truck. I held my nose as I passed, but the stench seemed to leach through my skin. It hit the back of my mouth like a tiny fist, triggering my gag reflex. Even after I'd left the truck half a block behind, the odor hung with me.

"Hurry," Ardie called from the shade of the theater's marquee. "Doug's holding seats."

And he was. A few rows from the rear he stood guard over two vacant seats next to Gertrude and Aston. He was grinning like a hyena. "Did you listen to the cooking disaster?"

"You bet." I returned his grin. "It was—"

"Excruciating," Ardie said.

"Painful," Gertrude agreed. "I felt so sorry for Brenda."

Doug's grin faded. I clapped a hand over my lips. I should have known Gertrude would see beyond the humor and sympathize with her colleague.

"After all the humiliation on the air, Brenda drove Jake to the emergency room," she continued. "And then she paid what the insurance didn't cover to have his prescription filled."

Because, as usual, Jake probably didn't have more than a few bucks in his wallet and was overdrawn at the bank. "I bet he said he'd pay her back." I spoke from past experience. "And I further bet he never will."

"You won't get anyone to take those bets," Doug assured me.

Aston snorted. "Brenda got what was coming to her."

I agreed with part of that. After all, it was common knowledge that Jake was the proverbial loose cannon. And I'd warned her about the state of the kitchen. So she should have realized things could go sideways. But unless you had a world-class imagination and/or significant prior experience with Jake, it was hard to grasp exactly how far sideways things could go.

And I was reminded again of the old saying about pride that goeth before a fall. If Brenda hadn't jumped at the opportunity so quickly and been so—

"Attention everyone," a man called from the stage. He was tall and pale. The bags under his eyes, the stubble on his chin, and the wrinkles on his cheeks made me wonder if he'd slept more than a few hours a night for the past week. I guessed being head of the teachers' union wasn't up there on the relaxation scale alongside lounging in a balcony suite on an all-expenses-paid cruise. In fact, I guessed it was at the bottom of the scale along with barely surviving a shipwreck and swimming to shore through shark-infested waters.

"Please take your seats. Let's get started. We have a lot to discuss."

Item one was whether to return to the picket line when the meeting concluded.

Chapter 21

The first person to speak was a second-grade teacher with a voice so sweet you could spoon it on ice cream and add nuts and a cherry to create a sundae. "I feel like we should hold back for at least another day. We should show respect for Marybeth Potter. Wherever she may be. She could be going through a horrible ordeal. She could be—"

Her voice broke and she wiped her eyes with a tissue.

Aston shot to his feet, feet clad in moccasins that appeared to have been gnawed on by rats, crusted with mud, and packed away wet. "When did she show respect for us? When did she talk about teachers without looking like she'd got hold of a rancid strip of elk jerky and needed to puke it up?"

Several younger teachers half stood and turned to see the man who could use such descriptive language. Several older teachers rolled their eyes. Doug ducked and pretended to search for something on the floor.

"I've come across grizzlies with a stronger sense of compassion," Aston went on. "I've seen wolverines care more about community. I—"

Ardie and Gertrude grabbed the sleeves of his flannel shirt. The aged fabric ripped as they pulled him down. It ripped more as he thrashed in their grip. "They get it," Gertrude said.

"You don't have to list every creature in the wilderness to make your point," Ardie added.

Aston jerked loose and glared at a shoulder-to-elbow tear in his left sleeve. "And you don't have to shred my clothes to make yours," he growled. "Marybeth Potter is a heartless harpy," he shouted to the audience. "She's a menace to society. She should be—"

Gertrude slapped a hand over his mouth. "We get it. They get it."

I glanced around and noted that almost everyone in the theater had turned to stare. Heat flashed up my cheeks and, taking my cue from Doug, I doubled over and hugged my knees.

Aston twisted and bucked. "Get your fist out of my face, woman," he raged in a mumble.

"She's trying to save you from yourself," Ardie insisted.

"And I'm trying to save this school district from—"

The rest of that sentence was so muffled I couldn't make it out.

Huddled as I was, I had only a dim view of the concrete floor, the tips of my sandals, and the bolts in the back of the seat ahead of me. But when I canted my head I saw past Doug's knees to the aisle, and I spotted two sets of feet. The feet wore heavy black shoes. The attached legs sported the navy uniform pants of the Reckless River Police Department.

Grunts and muffled warnings and threats signaled that Gertrude and Ardie were doing some serious grappling in their attempt to keep Aston muzzled.

One set of police feet turned in our direction and took a step closer. I wondered if the officers had heard all of

Aston's comments and were viewing him as a potential suspect in Marybeth Potter's disappearance.

I gripped Doug's knee to get his attention. "The police are here."

He swiveled for a look. Then he hissed, "Tell Ardie."

I turned toward Ardie, raised a few inches out of my hunch, and poked her in the side. "Cops. In the center aisle."

Ardie swiveled. "That's all we need." She swiveled back again. Aston yelped twice. Then, except for the first syllable of what I guessed was a curse, he was silent.

Doug and I uncurled by inches. Neither of us looked at Aston. Neither of us looked at the cops. He doodled on a yellow pad. I pretended to hunt for something in my purse.

The man on the stage banged a gavel on his podium and called for order. A woman in an official union T-shirt hustled down the aisle and confronted the officers, one of whom still faced my group, thumbs hooked in his belt, eyes narrowed, scalp gleaming through his close-cropped blond hair. Except for the words "union members only," I couldn't hear what she said, but in a moment the older officer shrugged and they both strolled out. She followed them to the top of the aisle and then stationed herself there as if to make sure they didn't return.

"Why are they here?" Doug asked me.

"No idea."

"Maybe a security precaution," Ardie offered. "I heard the union office got a couple of threats. Anonymous, of course. One guy called us anti-American for wanting more money."

"Really?" Doug raised his eyebrows. "I thought wanting more money is what capitalism is all about. And I thought capitalism was the Amer—"

"Quiet!" The union woman hissed.

Doug raised his hands in apology and the meeting got underway. It took an hour for the group to agree to hold off on picketing for another day and instead join other union groups at the park for a show of labor solidarity. "Grab some potluck stuff," Ardie instructed, "and we'll rendezvous on the side toward the river. West of the fountain."

The school librarian flagged me down in the theater lobby and, while I assured her I'd be available to sub for her again this year if I didn't get a position, I lost sight of my group. When I emerged into the daylight and headed toward my car, however, I had no difficulty spotting Aston.

He was the one surrounded by half a dozen police officers.

One of them leaned against a mailbox, alternately glancing at the garbage in the back of Aston's truck and jotting information on what I assumed was a citation form clipped in an aluminum holder. Another stood at the front of the truck, filling out a parking ticket. It appeared the remaining officers were questioning Aston. Based on his crossed arms, raised chin, and compressed lips, it appeared he was providing no answers and intended to stay the course.

I slipped into the doorway of an art gallery and pondered my own course. At the least, Aston would soon be the proud owner of a number of citations and a substantial ticket. It was within the realm of possibility that his truck would be impounded as a road hazard. Good citizen that I was, it would be logical that I take up a position where Aston could see me, wave to get his attention, and ask if I could help. Not monetarily, of course. But he might need a ride home.

I rejected the plan after only a few seconds of thought.

Aston would probably resent the assumption that he couldn't handle things himself and tell me to buzz off. The officers might also urge me to move along. Plus, at least one of them probably knew Dave and more than likely had heard about my tendency to be curious. No doubt he'd inform my significant other. That would result in a discussion we'd had many times before concerning the difference between being curious and sticking my nose in where it didn't belong.

(For the record, if there's a less productive discussion to be had in a relationship, I don't know what it is. And don't bring up the toilet seat issue. We resolved that the first week we lived together by deciding we'd leave the lid down, making work for both of us. And also don't mention the toilet paper issue. Cheese Puff resolved that by unspooling the roll Dave put in with the paper coming down over the front.)

But, let's get back to the story.

Choice two was to simply walk away, taking a roundabout path to my car. That, of course, would leave me hanging. I wouldn't know how this all played out.

Choice three was to stay in place and glean what I could. It was a choice that allowed me to feel I wasn't aggressively snoopy. It also allowed me to claim I was there for a friend if he needed me.

I went with it, squeezing farther into a slim triangle of shade and pretending to check my messages while really clicking off a few shots with my cell. Just as I got the third shot, the phone vibrated in my hand like an angry rattlesnake.

My sister's name lit up on the display. Well, it wasn't actually her name. This week I'd assigned her the label Lucrazy Bored-Ya. I take my fun at her expense in any little way I can.

No way was I about to call attention to myself by answering the phone while lurking in the doorway, so I let her leave a message. Of course I checked it as soon as she finished. "I should have expected you wouldn't answer," she ranted. "You have no sense of what's important and neither does your sorry excuse for a fiancé. He doesn't answer his phone either. It's apparent my project is on hold until this school board woman turns up. That leaves me no choice but to find her. As you know, I have superior investigative skills. I'll resolve this quickly. Then we can move on to more important things."

Wow.

I stared at the phone. Even for my sister this was over the top. On many levels. Least of all the claim to have superior investigative skills. That was clearly a jab at my success in bringing wrongdoers to justice.

(For the record, I'm well aware that some of my success has been accidental and/or the result of dumb luck that put me at the right place at the right time to catch a killer. A few times, though, I'd reached conclusions as a result of logical thinking and achieved success through careful planning. And, okay, I admit sometimes things blew up in my face and I needed a little rescuing.

But that's to be expected when you take on dangerous people and land in dangerous situations. I don't think my overall average should suffer because of it.)

Now, normally I'm not a competitive person. I've never gone all out to get better grades, make more money, keep my house cleaner, or diet my way to a size 4 before friends could reach similar goals. But I think I have a knack for picking loose the tangled threads of a mystery. And if strong suggestions are made that I leave things alone, or claims are made that I don't have what it takes, then I'm in. All in. And I'm going all out.

But, first things first. Before I could race my sister to the mystery-solving finish line, I had to know what was up with Aston.

Saving the message for incentive, I stuffed the phone in my pocket and concentrated on the scene unfolding before me.

Aston still stood with arms folded. The officers questioning him still jabbed fingers at him. The officers laboring over their paperwork still labored. It appeared they were throwing the book at Aston. Maybe several books.

A couple of teenage girls crossing the street paused to stare and the ticket-writing officer waved them on in a way that made it clear they shouldn't even think of lingering. I pressed myself tighter into the angle of the doorway, sucking in my stomach, clamping my arms to my sides, and taking only shallow breaths.

The officer with the citation pad tapped his pen on the sheaf of paper and walked around the truck, studying the tires. He stayed back a few feet in what I suspected was a futile attempt to avoid the worst of the stench. He wrote a little more and walked around again, this time checking the doors, hood, windshield, and tailgate. He wrote another line, then moved closer and surveyed the load. Shaking his head, he wrote another lengthy note. When he finished, he pinched his nose with his left hand and peered over the tailgate.

For a long moment he froze.

Then he called, “Check this out.”

Not one of his fellow officers hustled to his side. In fact, two didn’t move at all except to make dismissive hand gestures indicating they weren’t about to fall for his ploy to draw them into the heart of the funk. But when the others joined him and craned their necks to see the thing he pointed at, they sprang into action.

Two seized Aston’s arms and marched him to a vehicle. Another whipped out a cellphone and made a couple of quick calls. Another dashed to his car and returned with a roll of yellow tape.

It was the kind of tape I’d seen before.

It was the kind of yellow tape police officers use to cordon off crime scenes.

Chapter 22

In seconds the officer strung the crime scene tape around Aston's truck. Another made a call and, in a loud and excited voice, called for a detective and an evidence technician.

What the heck was in there?

I attempted to build a mental catalog of everything I'd seen yesterday as we tossed in trash bags from the rec center. Unfortunately, I discovered I'd successfully blocked most of what I'd seen. My only intense memory was of the stench.

But the truck was parked on the way to my car. Perhaps as I strolled by I could get a glimpse of what concerned the cops enough to take Aston into custody and treat his truck as a possible crime scene.

As I was studying the slant of the sidewalk and getting mentally set to move, the parking-ticket writer finally snapped his pad closed and glanced up and down the street. His gaze settled on me. I tightened all my muscles and held my breath.

But to no avail.

"Move along." He strode in my direction, with the kind of expression that indicated arguing would be not only futile, but also hazardous to my plans for the remainder of the day.

Planting himself in the center of the sidewalk, he cut off my route past the truck, and pointed in the opposite direction. "That way."

"Moving now." I gave one second's worth of thought to snapping a shot of Aston in the back of the patrol car. Then I abandoned the idea and scuttled off.

Realizing that spaces around the park would have been snapped up long ago, I decided to leave my car at the condo and walk. Dave was nowhere around and there were no messages on the landline's machine. Allison was still in bed, so I left a note on the table explaining where I was, where Cheese Puff was, and the options available for lunch. They were slimmer than the day before but that might make her a little more appreciative the next time I hit the supermarket and lugged home provisions. I checked the pantry and found that, unless I counted potato chip crumbs or stale peanuts or the few malted milk balls remaining in my stash, my potential contributions to the snackage supply at the park were nonexistent.

Grabbing a hat and checking that I had a few bucks in my purse, I set off on the mile-long hike to the park. I did it in stages, zipping through patches of sunlight and lingering in puddles of shade and in the air conditioned convenience market where I picked up a sack of cookies. The sack bore a banner claiming they were new, improved, and healthier.

Healthier than what?

I didn't ask the teenage clerk—he was engrossed in some kind of game on his phone and his scowl made it clear I should collect the change he dumped on the counter and leave as fast as my stubby legs would carry me. I considered the nuisance value in hanging around and making a series of small purchases to annoy him and demonstrate that his mood set the tone for his customers. In the end, however, I decided to save my energy for someone who truly deserved annoyance—like my sister.

Still, I pondered the healthier-than question as I tore open the bag and popped a cookie in my mouth to sustain me in my long march. Healthier than eating an entire stick of butter? Than stuffing a dozen doughnuts down my throat? Than drinking a bottle of absinthe? Than eating unwashed lettuce?

I was still building my list when the park came in view and I spotted Doug and a girl I recognized—as soon as I checked out her shoes—as Seleena Potter. The platform sandals were hot pink and high-heeled. Each sported about twenty feet of strap that crisscrossed her legs from ankles to thighs, ending well short of the hem of a black leather skirt so narrow it nearly qualified as a wide belt. A skimpy halter top, also in hot pink, completed her outfit.

She was holding a one-sided conversation with Doug, smiling, fluffing her streaked hair, waving a sheet of paper, thrusting her chest forward, and reaching out in an attempt to touch his arm.

Doug, hands deep in his pockets, backed away each time she reached. He repeatedly glanced left and right and then over his shoulder. Obviously a man in need of rescue.

Clutching the open bag of cookies, I jogged across the intersection and took a stand beside him. Holding the bag between them, I tipped the opening toward Doug. "Cookie?"

"Thanks." He grasped the sack like it was the only thing between him and a fall over the rim of the Grand Canyon.

Seleena's smile morphed to a frown. "Excuse me," she said in a snarky voice.

"Oh, I'm sorry." I went for a syrupy tone with a hint of sarcasm. "Would you like a cookie, Seleena?"

"We were *having* a *conversation*," she said with emphasis sprinkled here and there. "I have something very important to show Mr. Whitman. Something about my mother."

My ears perked up.

(For the record, I've always found that to be a pretty strange expression. First, I have no idea which muscles to engage to do that. Since I have yet to master the art of raising one eyebrow, I'm not sure I have what it takes to perk. And second, whenever I hear perk I think of coffee, or of someone who is perky. Too much perking can result in coffee stronger than I like it. Ditto for perkiness. Too much and I feel like there's a fly buzzing around my head. As the perky level increases, so does my desire to swat.)

"What is it?" I reached for the paper.

"It was in our mailbox." Seleena thrust it behind her back. "It's about what happened to my mother. I think it's very important. That's why I want Mr. Whitman to see it. Not you."

I was about to ask why she hadn't taken the note to the police, when Doug spoke up. His voice was soothing, his verbal pace slow. "I'm sure it's very important, Seleena. But I think Barbara, uh, Ms. Reed should see it."

Seleena scowled at me. "Why?"

"She has a lot of experience with the law," Doug said. "And her partner is a detective."

Seleena brought the paper from behind her back, fingers clutching and wrinkling it. I wondered how long she'd had it and if she was destroying fingerprints or other evidence. Again, I wondered why she hadn't called the police. Surely detectives would have left her their cards and phone numbers after they interviewed her. Surely someone checked in with her regularly to see if she'd heard anything or recalled something she hadn't mentioned earlier.

"If you won't show it to Ms. Reed, then take it to him." Doug pointed along the street to a Reckless River police car pulling up to the curb.

"But I wanted you to see it before anyone else," she said in a little-girl whine.

Doug crossed his arms. "I'm not qualified to look at it."

And I was?

The answer to that was, as you well know, negative. But my curiosity was now far beyond overdrive. I dug a tissue from my purse and used it to snatch the paper. Seleena made a grab for it, but I turned aside and blocked her with an elbow.

The words on the page were printed with thick lines of pencil that slanted left and then right and then left once more. They also wavered here and there. Was the person who jotted them sloppy, rushed for time, or trying to make it difficult to tell which hand was dominant?

"We'll release your mother when she pays $10,000." I frowned and read that number aloud once more. "And agrees to vote for all the union demands."

Eeek.

The demand for ransom money could have come from anyone. Well, from anyone who would settle for what I considered a paltry amount of money considering the risk involved. But the demand for union support seemed more likely to originate with someone who had skin in that game. Meaning a teacher. Meaning, maybe, someone like Aston Marsden.

"We need to get that to the police right away." Doug turned to Seleena. "Come with us. They'll want to talk to you."

"Why?" She reached for his arm. "I don't want to talk to them again. They just keep asking the same questions over and over. Can't you tell them it was in the mailbox?"

"No." I stepped between them as Doug, displaying the kind of footwork generally seen in a boxing ring, danced aside. "He can't. He's not the one who found it." I nodded toward the police car and the officer now leaning against its fender. "Let's go."

She made a sound that was part sigh and part whine, pouted, fluffed her hair, and finally took off at a slow and wobbling pace. I blamed her speed—or lack of it—partly on her attitude and partly on the sandals. But I gave her credit for being able to walk in them at all. After three steps I'd succumb to the force of gravity and be lying on the sidewalk clutching a sprained ankle and cursing the trends and temptations of fashion.

The young officer—sunburned and a little sweaty—pasted on a narrow-eyed expression of suspicion as we approached. He read the note I held by the tissue while I explained. Then he ordered us to remain where we were and called for Detective Charles Atwell.

If you've been following the story of my life, you know Atwell and I met when I was suspected of murdering Henry Stoddard, a history teacher at Captain Meriwether High School. Stoddard was as well liked as bubonic plague, so there were plenty of other suspects. But Atwell liked me best. Over the course of several days he grilled me like a rack of ribs at a summer barbecue.

That he was just doing his job is an age-old excuse. I usually don't buy it. But as I got to know Atwell, and recognized he wasn't much of a color-outside-the-lines kind of guy, I accepted that. I even forgave him a little. But I haven't forgotten. Every time I see him, I recall my fear that circumstantial evidence would send me to jail. And, since Atwell is Dave's buddy, I see more of him than I'd like.

It also doesn't help our rocky relationship that his pride suffered a couple of deep wounds when I provided insight and ideas that helped him catch at least one killer. In my experience, physical wounds sometimes heal faster than injuries to the ego.

So, when he drove up a few minutes later, I wasn't surprised to see his expression—half disgust and half martyred acceptance. It was clear he wasn't feeling the love, either.

Chapter 23

Atwell snapped open a plastic bag and held it out. I slid the paper inside and he studied it for a moment. Then his frown deepened and he asked, "What's your role in this?"

"When Seleena Potter said the note she found in her mailbox concerned her mother, I knew it should go to the police. She was crumpling it, so I took it from her. I used the tissue so I wouldn't leave prints. Then I walked with her to this officer and told him what it was. He instructed me to hold it until you arrived."

Atwell gave a curt nod and I told myself to leave it at that.

But, of course, I didn't.

"So, that's my role. It's only a small supporting role in this unfolding drama," I quipped. "Probably not even enough for an Oscar nomination."

"Cut the attempt at humor." He turned to Doug. "Who are you?"

"Doug Whitman. I teach English at Captain Meriwether."

"And you're here because?"

Doug glanced over his shoulder at the crowd in the park. "I came for the union celebration."

"And your ro—?" Atwell grimaced. "And your part in this is?"

"I'd just arrived at the park—about 20 minutes ago—when Seleena appeared and showed me the note."

"Appeared?"

"Poor verb choice," Doug said, his words crashing and colliding. "She didn't appear. Not like, you know, a magician in a puff of smoke. See, I was coming along the sidewalk and she called out from the crosswalk and—"

Atwell made a chopping motion and turned his icy gaze on Seleena. "Why?"

"Huh?"

"Why bring the note to him?"

Seleena blushed and combed her long hair with her fingers. "I knew he'd know what to do."

Atwell's jaw dropped and he shook the plastic bag in her face. "And you didn't? Your mother is missing, you find this in your mailbox, and you have no idea what to do with it?"

"Um, no."

"Amazing! You didn't realize this is vital? You didn't realize it's a ransom note? You didn't have a clue that you should bring it to the police immediately?"

"I guess." She twirled a strand of hair and cast a sidelong glance at Doug.

"You guess you had a clue?"

"I guess. But I wasn't sure, you know? And I thought if I showed it to Mr. Whitman he'd tell me, you know, if I was right and how to call the police and what to say and all."

Atwell gaped, started to speak, and stuck with the gape.

But I got it.

And from the way Doug took a couple of quick steps to the rear, I saw that he did too.

Seleena had cast herself in a leading dramatic role for the benefit of a one-man audience. To her the note was a prop. It was central to the scene she'd written in her head.

Atwell closed his mouth with an audible snap and shook his head as if trying to wake from a nightmare. "Is lack of intelligence a teenage thing?" he asked me.

"Not necessarily," I hedged. "I could name a few polit—"

"A girl thing?"

"That's sexist and insulting." I raised my voice and let my irritation show. "And why are you asking me about intelligence? I'm not an expert in that field."

He snorted. "Since when has lack of expertise stopped you from offering an opinion in any field?"

Aha.

That may have sounded insulting to you, but I read it as more of a reaction to feeling threatened by me. That, however, was his problem, not mine. So I didn't respond. I did gloat. But silently.

"All right." He pointed to Seleena. "You, get in the car. You're coming with me to go over this from the beginning."

He pointed at me and Doug. "You two, buzz off."

Seleena turned a pleading gaze on Doug. "Can Mr. Whitman come with me?"

"No," Doug yelped.

"No," Atwell seconded.

Seleena pouted. "But I want him to. Aren't I supposed to have a grown-up with me?"

"You're 18, aren't you?" I asked.

"Nineteen," she said with smug pride. "Last month."

"Then I'm pretty sure you're considered an adult," I told her in a voice short on empathy, sympathy, compassion, or patience.

"You're not in trouble," Doug added in a kinder voice.

"Well, not in a whole lot of trouble. Not the kind of trouble where you need a lawyer," I amended after taking in Atwell's scowl. "You should have called the police the second you saw the note. You shouldn't have carried it around getting your fingerprints all over it and contaminating possible trace evidence."

Atwell opened his mouth, but I rushed on. "But what's done is done, so Detective Atwell probably won't harp on that too much. He'll ask you how you found the note and if there was an envelope and if you have any ideas about who might have sent it, and, uh, stuff like that."

"But I don't know anything." She pressed her hands together as if in prayer, fingertips aimed at Doug. "They want money. A lot of money. Where do I get it? Where do I take it? Who do I give it to? When do I get my mother back?"

Doug performed another backward jig.

"You'll get another note," I said. At least that's the way it happened on TV crime shows. Although I suspected not everything on those shows was completely factual. "Or maybe you'll get a phone call."

Atwell's scowl deepened.

"And I'm sure the police will help you with everything," I continued in my chirpiest voice. "They're trained for situations like this. And the note didn't warn you not to contact them. It didn't say your mother would be hurt if you did."

And that seemed odd because on TV the notes almost always said not to go to the police or the hostage would get hurt. Maybe the kidnapper didn't watch TV or read mysteries or thrillers and wasn't aware of the way things are "supposed" to be done. Or maybe the kidnapper was confident he or she could outwit the cops.

I watched Atwell reread the note. Twice. Perhaps he was hoping he'd overlooked the bit that told Seleena to steer clear of the cops or she'd never see her mother again. Perhaps he was searching for a reason to bow out or hand the investigation off to someone else.

He made a snarly-grunty noise that made me think of a tiger with a sore paw. He followed that up with an expression of disgust that swept across Doug and Seleena and settled on me like a wet wool coat in a cold rain. I had no doubt that he'd be on the horn to Dave before the day was over, spewing out his side of the story. I also had no doubt his side would coincide with my version only in terms of date, time, and geography.

"I'm scared." Tears leaked from Seleena's eyes. "I'm scared for my mother. I'm scared she'll never come home again. I'll scared I'll be all alone."

She reached out for Doug who, crablike, scuttled aside. I snatched the sack of cookies from him before he got too far. "The police will find your mother," I told Seleena with what I hoped sounded like genuine confidence. I backed that up with a glare aimed at Atwell.

"But what if they don't?" Arms extended, she moved toward Doug again. "What if—?"

"Your father will be there for you." Doug scuttled behind me. "You once told me he's a nice guy."

“He’s okay. But he lives in an apartment.” She said the last word with a shudder and a tone of fear and loathing you might employ when referring to Alcatraz or the Black Hole of Calcutta.

Before I could leap to the defense of apartment living, she blinked away her tears and went on. “The apartment doesn’t even have a pool. And he hardly makes any money compared to my mother. And he says he doesn’t care if he’s not rich because he has all he needs and he’s happy that way.”

“Enough,” Atwell growled. “We’re wasting time. Let’s go.”

Seleena cast one more entreating glance at Doug.

He shook his head.

She blinked a few more tears onto her lashes, but didn’t make another move on Doug.

I held the sack of cookies toward Atwell. “Want a snack for the road?”

“No. I want you to hit the road.”

“His bark is worse than his bite,” I said as I offered the sack to Seleena.

She pushed the bag aside. “I don’t like that kind.”

“I do.” Doug seized the bag with both hands like a trapeze artist latching on to a bar after an aerial somersault. “Let’s go, Barb.”

I favored Atwell with a two-finger wave and followed Doug. We threaded our way through the crowd to where the rest of the gang, including Brenda, sat on a quilt made out of what appeared to be socks and scarves and gym shorts. I suspected Ardie, never one to toss anything that could be reused, had intercepted the contents of the Captain Meriwether lost and found cabinet as the custodians carried items to the trash bins. She'd probably washed what could be salvaged for the Family Support Room and quilted the rest.

Plastic containers, not unlike those we'd removed from the rec center refrigerator yesterday, were piled in the center of the quilt. Not one was open and I suspected they'd remain closed until Brenda popped their tops. At the moment, arms and hands dabbed with ointment, she was regaling Gertrude and Ardie with her version of the on-air debacle. From Gertrude's glazed eyes and Ardie's stifled yawn, I guessed the story had been repeated several times and achieved epic proportions.

Clearly, it was time for a fresh topic of conversation.

And I had just the thing.

Chapter 24

"Aston's been arrested," I announced.

After a round of gasping, the expected questions followed. I answered as best I could. "I don't know why, but I'm pretty sure it has to do with something in his truck. The cops were citing him for what I guess were parking and load violations and one of them spotted something in with all the other crud."

"You mean he didn't go to the dump like he said he would?" Ardie asked.

I rolled my eyes to make it clear I didn't answer stupid questions unless I was being paid. Well paid.

She apologized by smacking herself on the forehead.

"What did they see?" Gertrude asked.

"I don't know. It was in the rear. By the tailgate." I turned my palms up. "That's all I know. I wanted to sidle by and see if I could get a peek, but they hung crime scene tape around it and chased me off."

"Could it have something to do with the scraps of fur? Or the bones?" Doug lowered himself to a corner of the quilt. "Maybe Aston shot an endangered animal."

"Aston would never do that." Brenda popped to her feet and planted her hands on her hips. "Never."

"Not on purpose," Gertrude agreed. "But what if a shot went wild and—?"

"Aston's shots never go wild," Brenda fumed. "Never."

I wouldn't bet my condo on that. Aston was a good shot but, in the spirit of historical accuracy, he often used replica firearms. Like the originals, they weren't noted for their accuracy over any great distance. And if he set traps while channeling a fur trader, who knew what might have ended up between the jaws.

On the other hand, he was an outspoken supporter of legislation to protect endangered species. And he had a strong moral code. If he killed a creature threatened with extinction, he'd turn himself in.

"He needs a lawyer. He needs bail." Brenda stooped and snatched up a purse the size of the spare tire in my trunk. "He needs me!"

She shoved her way into the swelling crowd, heading for the police station a few blocks from the park, and calling over her shoulder. "Eat all you want."

"Don't worry," Ardie called. "We will."

"And it won't take long," Doug said, "since all we want is for the stuff to disappear."

"We'll take care of cleaning up the containers," Gertrude called.

Brenda waved over her shoulder to show she'd heard. Then she was lost in the crowd.

Gertrude nodded toward a row of garbage bins beside a park kiosk. "We'll take care of cleaning up the containers, cleaning them right into the trash."

"Contents unseen?" Doug asked.

"That's the best way." Ardie opened her purse and pulled out a folded black plastic garbage bag. "You never know when you'll need to do a little picking up and disposing." She pointed at a container with a bulging lid. "Start with that one. It has 'botulism' written all over it."

"Back to Aston," Gertrude prompted after we'd consigned Brenda's offerings to the bag and Doug had slung it in a container far from where we sat. "What else was in that truck? What could the cops be interested in?"

Ardie, Doug, and I formed a square with Gertrude and leaned in close, creating a human shield to soften the noise of the crowd swirling around the quilt. We reeled off what we remembered—furniture and kitchenware, hides, bones, a tent, fish, fishing lines and a net, a lampshade, a rake, and—

"Shoes!" Ardie's eyes widened. "A pair of women's shoes."

"That's right," Doug agreed. "They were brown."

"With gold buckles," I added. "And low heels. And square toes."

"They were polished," Ardie finished. "They looked almost new."

We were all silent for a few moments and then Gertrude said, "Maybe they were Brenda's shoes. Maybe she left them at his house the last time they broke up."

Silence closed in again and then Ardie said in a soft and tentative voice, "Brenda wears higher heels. Much higher."

"Well, maybe they belong to his sister," Gertrude said.

"Doesn't have one," Ardie informed her.

"Okay, maybe another woman."

"Doubtful," I said.

Gertrude nodded. "Maybe a friend."

"Aston's friends share his love of reenacting," Doug said. "They wear boots or moccasins."

"Maybe he found them on the street. Or maybe . . ."

Gertrude's voice trailed away and, after another round of silence, Ardie leaned closer and whispered what I was thinking. "Maybe the shoes belonged to Marybeth Potter."

Doug nodded slowly.

"I can't believe Aston would—" Gertrude put a hand to her throat. "But . . ."

"But what?" we asked as a chorus.

"Well, he and Marybeth Potter have history."

"History?" Ardie and I asked.

"History?" Doug echoed. "Bad history? Like war?"

"I guess it's kind of a war. She wants him fired."

"Why?" Ardie asked.

"For what?" I added.

"Mostly for being himself. When she was new on the board and not up on the limits of her authority, she walked by his classroom on one of those community tours. Jessica Flint—she was assistant principal back then—tried to hurry things along, but once Marybeth Potter got a peek in his room, she wouldn't budge. The more she stared at him, the angrier she got."

"Was it because of what he was wearing?" Doug guessed.

"Was it the fringed buckskin? The mountain lion pelt cape?" I reeled off other items of his wardrobe—some of them ancient and reeking of rancid grease and campfire smoke, some made of faux fur and often matted with mud or stained with coffee. "The knee-high boots with the skunk stripes. The chaps? The bear claw necklace?"

"All I know is he had on some kind of a fur hat with dangling tails and feathers." Gertrude fluttered her fingers along the sides of her face. "They were supposed to keep bugs away. He said it was a guaranteed attention-getter when he lectured about the settlement of the west. Anyway, Marybeth Potter found it repulsive and ordered Jerome Morrow to tear up Aston's contract immediately and see he was escorted from the building and never allowed back on school grounds."

"Wow," I said, "that's harsh."

"And beyond the valley of overreaction," Ardie added.

"Wait." Doug held up a hand. "Did I hear you correctly? She actually found Jerome Morrow?"

A good question. Morrow had been known as the invisible principal. I'd spotted him a few times, but only from a distance. Some school employees had never seen him. A few had questioned whether he existed at all.

"She found Jerome Morrow," Doug marveled.

"Not exactly," Gertrude clarified. "She found his office and unloaded on the Chillster."

I laughed. "That was a dumb move."

"Right up there with taking delivery of the Trojan horse," Doug agreed.

"Definitely. Big Chill explained—not all that patiently—about teachers' contracts and reasons for terminating those contracts, including a drop in enrollment or consecutive bad evaluations."

From the school gossip grapevine I knew Aston's evaluations, while never gold-standard, came in above the danger zone. "And then?"

"And then Marybeth Potter started searching for loopholes. And for evidence his evaluations were faulty or biased. She put the word out she wanted to hear about anything Aston did that crossed the line—even by a millimeter."

I had no trouble recalling a couple of questionable incidents from the previous school year.

Neither did Doug. “Aston straddles the line about once a day.”

“Yes,” Gertrude agreed, “but so far no one’s gone running to the board.”

“What happens inside the walls of Captain Meriwether High School stays there,” Ardie said.

“But Aston wasn’t inside the school when he said all those incendiary things the day we were picketing,” I pointed out. “And he spouted off at the meeting this morning. Two police officers were only a few feet away. They heard every word.”

“I’m sure he isn’t responsible for whatever has happened to her.” Ardie patted my shoulder. “Aston shoots his mouth off a lot, but I don’t think he’d hurt anyone.”

“Unless he was defending himself,” Doug added in a firm voice.

“Or protecting the herd,” Ardie mused.

I was picturing us as the herd and Marybeth Potter as a threat to our safety when a new voice said, “Interesting.”

I groaned.

How long had Stan Stewart been lurking and listening? I torqued my neck, shaded my eyes, and peered into a glare of sunlight. “What was that about shoes?” he asked. “You got pretty quiet after that and I didn’t hear much until that bit about protecting the herd.”

“We didn’t want you to hear us,” Ardie said.

“We were speculating,” Doug insisted. “Discussing possibilities. Not facts.”

"Well," Stewart tapped his notepad with a pen that appeared to have made a trip through a meat grinder, "it's a fact that your buddy Aston Marsden is being questioned right now. And it's a fact his truck was impounded and towed off to be checked for evidence. And it's a fact he had a pair of women's shoes that smart money says weren't his. Unless he enjoys cross-dressing."

Despite efforts to keep my mind blank, my imagination ran amok, manufacturing a mental portrait of Aston in those shoes, a fringed skirt, a frilly pink blouse, long braids, fluffy bangs, and his scraggly beard. A series of snorts and snuffles told me the others were visualizing similar images.

"I'll assume he isn't." Stewart tapped the pad again. "I need background. Accurate background. You all worked with him. What can you tell me about him? As a person and as a teacher."

What we could tell him about Aston was colorful, but it might not help his cause.

"He took part in historical reenactments all over the Northwest," I said. "He portrayed mountain men and pathfinders and military figures. He strove for authenticity, down to the tiniest details, even to eating the same kind of food they ate."

I didn't mention that he often brought some of that food to school, slicing off moldy sections or pounding petrified biscuits on the table to break them into bits he could swallow. I also didn't mention the jar of bear grease he'd acquired with the idea of somehow demonstrating changes in air pressure and thus forecasting the weather. And I certainly didn't mention how the jar broke and the rancid grease created a gag-inducing stench while I subbed in his classroom on a hot day.

"Aston loves history," Gertrude said. "He makes it come alive in the classroom by dressing in character. Once he came as General Grant."

She stopped short of mentioning the bit where his quest for authenticity resulted in the evacuation of the building because smoke from the cigar he lit up to round out the character set off the fire alarm.

"He liked hands-on projects. His classes built replicas of log cabins and keelboats and encampments," Doug said.

He also stopped before adding that class projects from many years past were piled on bookshelves and stacked in closets collecting dust and providing havens for bugs and mice.

Ardie cast a sly glance in my direction. "He has a unique approach to lesson planning."

Meaning he didn't make lesson plans more detailed than a word or two jotted on an old lunch sack. On the plus side, it didn't take long to read his plans, and the lack of complexity made them easier to follow than many others I'd encountered.

"He's an interesting guy," I offered.

"Unique," Doug agreed.

"One of a kind," Gertrude chimed in.

Stewart narrowed his eyes. "Why do I think there's an entire encyclopedia of information you're not sharing?"

Chapter 25

"You think like that because you have a suspicious nature," I suggested. "Because you're an investigative reporter. You always begin an interview with the assumption people won't tell you the truth. Or at least not the whole truth."

Stewart opened his mouth as if to deny the charges. Then he scowled, pocketed his pen and pad, and stalked off in the direction of the cop shop. Before he was sucked into the crowd, he passed Deming Featherstone who raised a hand in greeting. Stewart didn't respond and Deming, hand still in the air, stumbled onward.

I waved and motioned him over. "He's on a mission," I assured Deming when he reached our group. "Don't take it personally. If you aren't a source, you cease to exist." I patted the quilt. "Sit and tell us all about Jake. And Dario. Was he furious?"

"Yes." Deming sat, took a cookie from the sack, glanced at his burgeoning belly, glanced at the claims of healthiness on the package, and bit off half the treat. "And no."

"Well, that's clear as mud," Ardie said.

Deming chewed, wrinkled his nose, and swallowed. "Not worth the calories." He tossed the remains of the cookie toward a squirrel observing us while clinging to a nearby maple. The squirrel eyed it then dashed up the tree.

"Dario's reaction?" I prompted. "Clarification?"

"Okay, so Dario was mad because he didn't know about the cooking debacle until he got a call from a feature writer at the paper looking for a comment. He snapped at me—and I don't blame him a bit—but then he read through the e-mails we got." Deming wiped cookie crumbs from the corner of his mouth. "People loved it. They want us to rerun it so their friends can hear it. Six women called and volunteered to have Jake come to their homes to cook with them. At least a dozen people suggested we make it a regular feature. One guy says we should call it 'Mistakes with Jake' and have him tackle other things, like repairing electric cables and fixing clogged sinks."

"You'd never be short of material," I assured him.

"Don't I know. It would probably double our ratings in a week. But someone could be seriously injured."

"Someone besides Jake?" I asked.

"Right." Deming gave a slight nod of agreement before his better nature prevailed and he shook his head violently. "I mean, of course I don't want Jake to get hurt."

I grinned at his confusion. "Because if he's sidelined, the show goes down the tubes. And you're out of a job."

"Right." Deming's flush had faded, but now it returned with a vengeance, his skin fast approaching the color of borscht. "But that's not why I wouldn't want—"

"She's messing with you," Doug assured him. "But she has a point."

"A very clear point," Deming agreed. "Jake is a train wreck. Almost every day we have to issue an apology or a retraction. And after today's disaster our insurance might go up."

"And sooner or later someone might sue him," I added. "Over an unscripted remark."

"Of which I'm guessing there are dozens every week," Ardie said.

"Dozens," Deming agreed with a groan. "That's why we run a tape delay. But he's got an audience. And it's growing. Older woman think he's charming, and younger women think he's handsome."

"What about men?" Doug asked.

"Some think he's a BS artist who runs off at the mouth but they listen so they can make fun of his stupidity and feel superior. Others listen because they admire him." He spread his fingers. "Although I have no idea why."

"So unless Jake blows himself up," Gertrude mused, "your job is secure."

"As secure as any job in radio ever is," I said, remembering how I was downsized from my position during the recession. "But I think we can safely assume Deming won't be forced to relinquish his position as the number one coffee consumer in Reckless River anytime soon." I leaned over and tapped his watch. "Isn't it about time for a cup?"

"Um." Deming flushed once more.

"Run along," I told him.

He leaped to his feet, spun about to get his bearings, and took off like a rabbit racing to reach its burrow ahead of a fox.

"It's not just coffee he's running for, is it?" Ardie asked.

"There's a woman involved," Gertrude surmised.

"Got to be," Doug said with a wistful expression on his face. "Wish I had a reason to run."

"You will," Ardie and Gertrude and I said simultaneously. Doug was smart and handsome, but still getting over being jilted and not ready to jump back in the dating pool.

Ardie pointed to the bandstand. "Looks like the speechifying is about to begin."

Glancing in that direction, I spotted a portly legislator lumbering up the short flight of steps to the platform. I clamped my lips, but forgot it's possible to groan without opening your mouth.

"I second that," Ardie said. "He's more long-winded than a slow-moving hurricane."

Gertrude drew a sack of new and improved and better tasting puffs from a cloth shopping bag. "Fortunately we have cheesy snacks to tide us over until they wrap up."

As you well know, given enough cheesy snacks, I could tide myself through an entire day of speeches. But a single sack, and a relatively small one at that, wouldn't be nearly enough for this event.

I groaned again before I reminded myself the day, like so many others, wasn't all about me.

When I dragged myself home late that afternoon, Dave was asleep on the sofa. Despite a dozen minor cuts and bruises on his arms and face, he appeared cool and comfortable. I, on the other hand, was tired, dusty, and crispy around the edges thanks to sunbeams filtering through the leafy canopy above the park. Still, I was alert enough to see his sleep appeared to be deep and peaceful, not the fitful rest of a man who'd recently had a close encounter with my sister. I surmised that whatever Iz was doing to investigate the Marybeth Potter case hadn't involved grilling him in a relentless pursuit of information.

Allison was nowhere to be seen, and a search revealed no scribbled note on the table or counter. For a few seconds I wondered where she might be, then decided that was Dave's problem and he was welcome to it. With the stealth of a cat burglar, I tiptoed upstairs and took a cool shower. Recalling the stark state of our dining options when I returned to the main floor, I took my cell out to the deck, tapped the number of my favorite Chinese restaurant, and ordered a few favorites to be delivered.

As usual, I was low on cash—about as low as a wet-weather stream in the middle of a year-long drought—but Dave had thoughtfully left his wallet on the coffee table. I eased out a couple of twenties and tucked them in the pocket of my shorts.

"I could slap the cuffs on you for that," Dave said. His voice sounded like his face looked—rough and weathered.

"Promises, promises." I knelt by the sofa and gave him a serious kiss. "That's to keep you going on tomorrow's search."

I could almost see question marks form in his eyes.

"The search has been called off?"

His eyes seemed to frost over. "You know I can't talk to you about plans and procedures."

"Right. I know. I understand. Can you tell me if you turned up anything?"

He thought about that for a few seconds. "If by 'anything' you mean plastic bottles, aluminum cans, food wrappers, condoms, cigarette butts, and other junk, then yeah, we turned up a bunch of stuff."

"Did you have dogs?"

"Three. Trained trackers with lots of experience." He got a distant look in his eyes. "Made me miss the days when Lola and I were on the drug squad. We were a great team."

Until her allergies got worse. Until she broke a leg in a fall when Dave took her out on unauthorized search and rescue training. Until she was injured again when the department assigned her to a new partner and she ran off and was captured by drug dealers. Until Cheese Puff and Dario released her. Until Mrs. B paid for surgery and paid more to purchase a replacement. Until Lola "retired" to become a companion for Verna.

"Ever wish you were still on the drug squad?"

He thought for a moment. "I guess not. And I know Lola's better off where she is. I felt for those dogs when their handlers had them sniff Marybeth Potter's purse to get her scent."

"Why?"

"The thing reeked like the aftermath of an explosion in a perfume factory. One dog sneezed for a full minute."

"Poor dog. I heard she wore a lot of expensive fragrance."

"If that was expensive, then I hope I never have to sniff the cheap stuff."

"So, even with a strong scent to follow, the dogs found no trace of Marybeth Potter?"

He sat up, stretched, and considered again. "No apparent trace."

"There was nothing in those dilapidated houses along the road to the swimming hole?"

"Nothing except junk, mold, mildew, dust, mice, roaches, and evidence of teenage beer and sex parties."

I didn't need to ask what that evidence was.

"What about all the houses she had listed for sale? Did someone search those?"

He rolled his eyes. "We're trained professionals. And this isn't our first rodeo."

"Sorry." I planted another kiss. "Did they find anything when they searched? Anything you can tell me about."

He shook his head.

"Nothing you can tell me about? Or nothing that could have belonged to her? Or her kidnapper? Nothing that indicated she'd been held in one of those houses and then moved?"

He narrowed his eyes and gave me a glare that said I should stop trying to confuse him. The expression also made it clear he'd talked with his buddy Chuck Atwell and knew I'd read the ransom note. He made a sound, a rumbling puff of disgust. I assumed it was intended to remind me I'd been told not to get involved but, once again, had. "Yeah, Chuck said you delivered the note."

I shook my head. "That's as accurate as saying the source of the milk in the supermarket cooler is the truck driver who rolls it in on a dolly. What happened is that I took the note from Seleena Potter who either didn't care or seemed to have no idea about its importance or the need to preserve evidence. I delivered her and the note to an officer on duty at the park. He called your pal Atwell."

"I stand corrected," Dave said in a snarky voice.

"You're sitting," I pointed out in an attempt at humor.

"Whatever."

His tone was no less snarky, a sign I was unlikely to pry more information from him. Unless I lightened his mood by blinding him with fancy conversational footwork. "Apology accepted."

"Huh? What?"

"We don't have time to squabble. Dinner will be delivered in a few minutes and then you'll probably have to help your buddy Atwell interrogate Aston Marsden."

"He doesn't need help. Marsden isn't talk—"

Dave swore under his breath and gave me the narrow-eyed squint once more.

I refrained from smirking.

Sometimes it was far too easy to trap him.

On the other hand, sometimes it was far too easy for him to trap me.

"Food should be here soon."

Fluttering the bills, I dashed for the door and out to the parking lot where a girl about Allison's age was emerging from a car at least two years older. Her shiny black hair and spotless official restaurant T-shirt were in sharp contrast to the car's balding tires, rusty chrome, and scraped and dented fenders. She offered a white paper sack smelling of ginger and garlic, fried onions and wonton wrappers. Intoxicated by the fragrance and anxious to get inside and fill my rumbling stomach, I handed over both bills and told her to keep the change.

"If you're throwing money around," a voice said, "feel free to throw some my way."

Chapter 26

I turned to see my neighbor Jim, an all-around great guy with a beard like Father Christmas and a can-do attitude. "Did you land a teaching job?" he asked.

"No. Unless you know something I don't. Something you learned because you're tapped in to the school system pipeline through Big Chill."

Jim's cheeks—at least the bits visible above his beard—turned pink. "Wilhelmina does seem to have her finger on the pulse of the district."

"Finger? Heck, she's got all eight fingers and both thumbs on the main gossip artery. Plus she's got ears like a bat and a nose that can sniff out a rumor a mile away."

Jim cocked his head.

I rushed to add, "I say all that with admiration. The woman's my idol."

"She *is* a marvel," Jim agreed.

"But?"

"But what?"

I shrugged. "I don't know. It sounded like you wanted to put something else on the end of that sentence and caught yourself."

He scratched his chin with both hands. "I might could have."

I waited, holding the warm bag against my belly, keeping my lips clamped and swallowing the saliva pooling beneath my tongue. It was torture to breathe in the aromas of shrimp and spring rolls, but Jim had done me lots of favors over the years and he'd always been my ally against Bernina Burke. If he had something to say, I owed it to him to stand here and listen.

On the other hand, there was no law saying I couldn't sit inside and listen.

And eat at the same time.

I unfolded the top of the bag and let the aromas waft his way. "Would you like to join us for dinner?"

"Does a bear like honey?" Jim hesitated only a second before he hustled ahead to hold the door. "Sure you have enough?"

"Plenty. Unless my sister drops by."

Jim shaded his eyes and scanned the parking lot and the street beyond. "No sign of her."

"Yet," I cautioned. "But she has a way of popping up like a zit on prom night. Lock the door behind us."

Jim clicked the bolt and followed me down the hall. Dave was upright and drinking a beer.

"Jim's joining us."

Dave sighed with relief. "When I heard someone behind Barbara I was afraid it was her sister." He stuck out his hand to shake. "Good to see you."

"Especially because I'm not Iz?"

"Uh, well . . ."

Jim laughed. "No need to explain. Iz strikes terror into my heart too."

"And she's overdue." I opened the bag and pulled out half a dozen white cardboard containers. "She hasn't been by to annoy either of us for more than 24 hours."

"We'd better take precautions." Jim locked the sliding glass door to the deck and drew the drapes. "If she can't see us, we have half a chance of pretending we're not here."

"I think she has X-ray vision." I pulled plates from a cabinet in the kitchen and scooped up silverware and napkins. Before I got them all distributed, Dave had his plate loaded. Jim, always the gentleman, waited, holding my chair.

In turn, I waited until we finished eating to prod him. "The something you thought you 'might could' say, was it about Wilhelmina?"

Jim blushed again, brighter this time, and concentrated on using his fork to chase a grain of rice through a smear of soy sauce on his plate.

"I'll take that for a positive answer and guess again. Is it about your relationship?"

He gulped and stabbed at the rice.

"Are you wondering if you've reached a milestone? If you should move things to another level?"

Jim mashed the grain with the back of his fork.

"Maybe buy her a ring? Suggest you move in together?"

Dave thumped his empty beer bottle on the table. "Why don't you let him speak for himself?"

"Because he's not speaking."

"Maybe he's not speaking because you're not giving him a chance."

I stuck out my tongue.

Dave followed suit.

If you looked up "adult relationship" you wouldn't find a picture of us.

"Having trouble finding the words," Jim mumbled after a moment. "She's doing fine without me."

"Well if that's the case, I'm going on record as saying I think it's weird. And spooky." Dave shoved his chair back. "I'll be on the sofa. I hope that's far enough away to keep her from speaking for me."

Making a big show of glancing over his shoulder with what I imagined he intended as an expression of terror, he beat a retreat, clicked on the TV, and surfed channels.

While I waited for Jim to speak, I thought again about milestones and how, sometimes, they had a way of becoming millstones. Allison reached a milestone when she got her driver's license. But now we were subjected to bouts of high-energy pestering to let her borrow a car or to buy one for her. I'd reached a milestone when I completed the courses for my teaching degree. But now I often wondered if I wanted the stress of preparing lesson plans, grading, and being evaluated. Sure, the money was far superior to what I took home as a sub, but subbing gave me more flexibility, and so far—with a little help, an extra part-time job or two, and some creative budgeting—I'd managed to make ends meet.

"Where were we?" Jim asked.

I shook off my thoughts. "Talking about your relationship with Big Chill, and taking a step toward commitment."

"Right. We get along great. I don't want to mess that up." Jim combed his beard with his fingers. "Maybe I'm too old and set in my ways for marriage. I like having my own space."

"So do I." I glanced at the tiny rolling table/cabinet where I stored my laptop and filed bills and important papers. Once Dave and I had shared the cramped office by the front door, but now it was his man cave. I hadn't minded the sacrifice—hadn't really thought of it as all that much of a sacrifice—until this moment. Now I felt hemmed in, restricted, cheated. "But if you had enough space in a place you shared, maybe that wouldn't be an issue."

"Maybe." Jim sounded less than convinced.

"Do you think she expects you to propose? Or suggest you live together?"

"Don't know." He gave up on combing his beard and scratched the back of his head with both hands. "Maybe if I was the romantic type I could get a fix on that."

I reached across the table and patted his hand. "There's nothing wrong with not being the romantic type—whatever that is. You're a smart and practical man. She's a smart and practical woman."

"Real smart," he said with a note of pride.

"She just about runs the high school."

"Enjoys being in charge," he added.

I let him mull that for a few seconds before I said. "Maybe you shouldn't feel you have to take the next step just because you have a Y chromosome. Maybe you should ask her what she thinks, what she wants to do."

He returned to combing his beard. "That wouldn't make me look wishy-washy?"

"Not to her. She'd see you as being strong enough to be okay with not being in charge, as being sensitive to her needs. She'd think you were making it clear you view her as an equal partner in the relationship."

Jim did the head-scratch thing once more. "You sure?"

"She's sure," Dave called.

His tone implied he'd had enough of this impromptu counseling session. I suspected he feared I might try to engage him in a discussion of roles and feelings after Jim left. Dave could express his feelings, but not with ease, and seldom without appearing as if he was sucking in frigid air over the exposed nerve in a chipped tooth.

"I'm sure." I stood and began closing up boxes.

"Then I'll go try it." Jim pushed back his chair and hustled toward the door. "Right now. Before I chicken out."

Dave waited until the door closed to laugh and mutter, "Bet he doesn't do it. Bet he puts it off."

"Like you never chickened out of a relationship talk."

"I've postponed several and danced around a few," he claimed in a righteous voice. "But I never completely chickened out."

"Ha."

"What? When?"

Okay, so I couldn't think of a specific incident, but I was certain there were dozens. So I turned away to rinse plates and hit him with an answer that generally served me well in the classroom. "You know."

"I don't."

"You do."

The trick to "winning" this exchange or at least to ending with the score tied, was to avoid eye contact and say no more. I racked the plates in the dishwasher and wiped down the counters.

Dave muttered under his breath, scowled, and did some counting on his fingers. Then he turned up the volume on the TV.

When my cellphone rang, I leaped for it and, even though the display showed Stan Stewart's name, answered on the second ring.

"Your pal Marsden isn't talking," he said. "What do you know?"

An open-ended question if I ever heard one.

Chapter 27

I carried the phone into the pantry to make it tougher for Dave to listen in. He wouldn't admit it, unless it would save his life, but his curiosity was right up there with mine. And after he'd given me a hard time about the conversation with Jim, I was in the mood to tweak him.

Also, I'm always in the mood to tweak Stewart. "What do I know? Well, I know the earth isn't flat. I know the sun is hot. I know wrinkles aren't necessarily a sign of maturity. I know—"

"Enough."

"That's right. I know enough. Enough to hang up right now. Why? Because I'm not going to get anything from you in exchange for what I might have."

"That depends on what you have, doesn't it?"

He had a point. But basically, I had nothing—at least nothing I thought was worth trading, so I zipped my lips and waited him out. He lasted half a minute before he spit out a snippet of information. "Okay, those *were* Potter's shoes in the truck."

"Bah. That's a no-brainer. It's not a bargaining chip. It's not even the broken edge of a bargaining chip."

He grumbled for another half a minute before he gave me more. "Atwell is focusing on a narrow time frame late Saturday morning. Potter showed a house at 9:00 and dropped the clients off at 9:45. According to them, she took a call and agreed to meet someone for a showing at 10:00. No one knows where. Her office has no record of it. And her phone wasn't in her purse and hasn't turned up. They'll get the records—if they don't have them already—but I'm betting the call came from a burner."

So someone pretended to be interested in seeing a house Marybeth Potter had listed. And then? Kidnapped her? Killed her? The note Seleena found seemed to indicate she was alive, but . . .

"What time did the picketing start?" Stewart asked.

"Right around 11:00."

"Was Marsden there then?"

"I had the swap show," I hedged, "so I didn't get there until around 12:15."

"Yeah, yeah. What about Marsden? Do you know if he was there on time?"

If you've been following along, you know he wasn't. You also know he said he'd had "important" things to do.

(For the record, determining what is "important" can sometimes lead to sticky subjective arguments. I see it all the time in the classroom where kids have to make "important" phone calls to their friends while I'm giving instructions on a project. And I have no doubt that Aston and I wouldn't always agree on the definition. For example, he might think learning how to make pemmican and storing it for future meals was important. I would lean toward believing it was important to have enough cash on hand so I could order out and not have to rely on pemmican. But did I think the important thing he'd been doing involved Marybeth Potter? No. If it had, he would have tossed her shoes in the river instead of the back of his truck. So, someone was framing him.)

"Do you realize you're not speaking?" Stewart asked.

"Of course," I lied.

"Are you not speaking because Marsden wasn't there when the picketing started? Because you don't want to drop a dime on your buddy? Because you think he might be guilty?"

I hesitated again but decided if Stewart didn't get it from me he'd keep on poking and prodding. Sooner or later he'd get it from someone else. "Yes. Yes. No."

"He wasn't there at 11:00, huh?" I heard the scratching sound of pen on paper and the turning of a notebook page. "When did he turn up?"

"I don't know. Like I said, I didn't get there until 12:15. Gertrude Suttle would know." She'd also be the least likely to give him too much information. Ardie would also be a clam, and Doug would be cautious, but Brenda would spill all kinds of random details about Aston, possibly including details about their sex life.

I swallowed, fought a queasy feeling, and tried not to imagine any of those details. The effort resulted in failure. I don't know about you, but whenever I try not to imagine something, it explodes in my mind. It's like the scene in *Ghostbusters* where Dan Aykroyd's character fails to keep his mind blank at a critical moment and unleashes a marshmallow menace.

"What's so funny?" Stewart asked.

"Nothing." At least nothing that wouldn't take a lot of explanation if he'd never seen *Ghostbusters*. And if he had, I doubted he'd find the reference as amusing as I did.

"Are you holding out on me?"

I crossed my fingers. "Never."

"Hmmph. Why was Marsden late?"

To cut off questions about what Aston's important task might have been, I stuck to claiming lack of knowledge. "No idea."

"Is Marsden usually on time?"

"I don't know whether he's on time for his living history events, but he was on time for the rec center programs he helped with this summer. And he's always at school at least half an hour before the bell."

Except for the day he had to dig his way out of the cave he took up residence in when his roof started leaking during the March storms. But I didn't mention his choice of temporary residence or the collapse. Those who knew Aston hadn't been surprised by the misadventure, but Stewart might jump to the conclusion that Aston had stashed Marybeth Potter in that cave.

"What are you not telling me?"

"Nothing." Much. "Gotta go."

"Where? To do what?"

He barked out questions like he was a government interrogator grilling a suspected spy. Head swiveling, I glanced around the pantry like a cornered hedgehog. I was about to tell him it was none of his business when my gaze settled on a small pyramid of cans. Soup cans. Cans with colorful pictures on the labels. "I, uh, I have to go to the community vegetable garden," I blurted. "To pick tomatoes. And mushrooms. And, uh, dig potatoes. Before the, uh—"

I hesitated, glancing back and forth between chicken noodle and beef with barley. Chickens? Or cows? I went with egg layers. "Before the chickens get to them."

"Chickens? Someone is using their plot to keep chickens? That's got to be against regulations."

I heard the scratch of pen on paper and headed off his quest for a story that didn't exist. "No one's keeping them. These are rogue birds. Wild urban chickens."

"Feathered felons?" He snorted. "Really?"

"Really. Jailbirds. Except they're not in jail. Sometimes they're not sighted for days. They're clever. Like that cartoon roadrunner. The one the coyote never cat—"

"Stop BSing me. Those chickens are no more real than promises to cut taxes for the little guy. And I'm not buying the mushroom part of this either. I was down at the garden chasing a rumor of a marijuana grow last week, and I didn't see a single fungus."

"Mushrooms pop up fast."

"So do your excuses. And I've had enough. I've got places to go, people to see, stories to write."

And, without another word, he disconnected.

I turned to see Dave lounging in the pantry doorway, eyebrows raised. "Who was that?"

Since I had no idea how much he'd heard and what he could piece together, I decided to go with the truth and stick to it—until it became either inconvenient or incriminating. "Stan Stewart."

"Was he checking to see if you'd managed to weasel information out of me about the Potter case?"

"Yes." I brushed past Dave and set the phone on the counter. "I keep telling him to develop other sources like a real reporter, but he keeps pestering me. He won't believe you haven't told me anything."

"So you resorted to making up a story about marauding chickens?"

He said that as if he felt I shouldn't be proud of such creativity. "It got him off the phone, didn't it?"

Dave opened his mouth, but no snappy comeback emerged. After a moment he rubbed the stubble on his cheeks and announced with a leer, "Long day. I'm going to bed early. You coming?"

Even though I was miffed at him, I had no intention of turning down that invitation. *If* the coast was clear for unbridled pleasure. "Where's Allison?"

"At a party with Josh." He checked his watch. "She probably won't be home until curfew."

If then. Allison's pledge to stick to house rules had been eroding lately. I was leaving it to Dave to rein her in. And betting he wouldn't be yanking on those reins tonight.

He took my hand and started for the stairs, then halted. "While we're on the subject of possible interruptions, where's your entitled mutt?"

Shoot.

I hadn't exactly forgotten about Cheese Puff, but it was fair to say he wasn't at the center of the thoughts swirling in my mind. "He's next door."

"That sounded more like a question than an answer."

"Probably because I'm not sure he's there. He might be off somewhere with Mrs. B."

"As long as he's not here to get in my face."

(For the record, Dave swears he's not jealous of Cheese Puff, but there are times when I'm not sure he's honest about that. He is, however, honest about occasionally finding Cheese Puff annoying, especially when the little beast puts his mind to disrupting our attempts at quality time in the bedroom.)

"I agree it's nice to have the place to ourselves, but I should check on him."

I tried to free my hand, but Dave kept his grip. "Why? If he's with Mrs. Ballantine he's fine. In fact, he's usually more than fine."

"I know, but he did a face plant off the deck steps and Mrs. B freaked out and took him to the emergency clinic."

And I hadn't called to see how he was. I felt like I'd been dipped in a cold vat of congealed guilt. "I was sure he wasn't hurt. But maybe he was. I should have called. After all, he's my dog."

"On paper." Dave tugged me toward the stairs. "If he was hurt—and I mean really hurt, not just acting to get sympathy and treats—Mrs. Ballantine would have called you. He's probably milking a minor limp and reminding himself to whine in between taking bites of his own miniature sirloin steak."

"Still, I should check."

Dave groaned. "Why? Mrs. B wouldn't put him out on the street."

"No, but—"

"She'll think you're not as indulgent and over-protective as she is?"

He'd pretty much nailed it, but no way would I admit to that. "Like you said, my name is on his license. And, uh, if I go get him, we can be sure Mrs. B won't bring him over while we're—"

"Then go." Dave released my hand. "Go."

"I'll be back in a flash."

"Probably the slowest flash in the history of flashes," he muttered.

No doubt he'd nailed that too. Once or twice in the course of my relationship with Mrs. B I might have managed to be in and out of her condo in less than 15 minutes. But I couldn't recall when. And I suspected a few of those short visits were when she was on her way out the door. Or perhaps wasn't even home.

"I'm going to shower the grime from my magnificent body." Dave raised his arms and flexed his muscles. "Meet me between the sheets in ten minutes."

I blew him a kiss and set off.

Chapter 28

I had every intention of returning quickly.

But I was a mere three steps onto the deck when my cellphone vibrated against my hip.

In a moment of foolhardiness, I answered without checking the display.

Fortunately, the person on the other end wasn't my sister. But Iz was the topic of conversation.

"Was your sister raised by wolves?" Big Chill asked.

"No. But only because wolves have standards," I quipped. "What did she do?"

"Tried to grill me like a flank steak. Wanted information on Aston Marsden. Wanted to know if I thought he was unstable, if he believed he was a law onto himself, if there was a special place he camped or hunted where he might have built a shelter of some kind where he could hold a prisoner."

Shoot.

Iz knew the cops had picked up Aston. And probably knew he wasn't talking. She was trying to get evidence to nail him for Marybeth Potter's disappearance.

"What did you tell her?"

"To mind her own business. Even if I suspected Aston of kidnapping Marybeth Potter—which I don't—I wouldn't tell anyone without a badge." She paused for a moment, and then said, "Except you. I'd tell you because you have a knack for getting the wrong person off the hook and the right person behind bars. It's kind of a clumsy knack at times, but I guess if you stretch the definition you could still call it a knack."

That might not seem like much of a compliment to you, but from Big Chill it was high praise. "Thanks."

"But I don't know a thing about Aston's wilderness activities. And I don't want to. What I do know is your sister is a pain in the behind. A gigantic pain."

She disconnected before I could agree, apologize, sympathize, or turn the conversation to her relationship with Jim.

I spent a few minutes wondering about other ways Iz would attempt to get information. I doubted she had contacts in law enforcement. She'd made a career out of flaunting rules and regulations, thumbing her nose at police, celebrating her arrests, and crowing about the times when charges against her were dropped or negotiated away. Dave and Atwell would have put out the don't-cooperate word and I guessed there would have been no arguments about heeding it.

She'd probably try Stan Stewart before long, but I doubted he'd tell her anything. Unless it was in trade for something she knew and he didn't.

The thought created a cold flutter in my gut.

What if I was wrong about my sister's abilities?

What if Iz was able to find out things I couldn't?

What if she found Marybeth Potter?

What if she captured the kidnapper?

I inhaled a scream of anguish.

I'd live that down about the time the sun blinked out.

Seething, I crossed the deck, and spent a few minutes calming my mind by gazing through the growing twilight at the Columbia River. Imagining my sister handcuffed and floating out to sea helped bring me back around to considering the fate and present location of Marybeth Potter.

Dumping someone—alive or dead—in the river wouldn't be all that difficult, especially if that person was knocked out or tied up or no longer living. Marybeth Potter could have been tossed into the current from any of a dozen close-by and easy-to-reach locations. Or she could have been dumped elsewhere, like in steep terrain along the many streams that ran through Reckless River's greenbelts. Offhand I could think of at least three homes under construction along the rim of one ravine. On a holiday-weekend Saturday, it would take only a few minutes to slip a car in among stacks of bricks and mounds of earth, drag a body through what would become the back yard, and tumble it down the slope.

But holding Marybeth Potter hostage somewhere and keeping her alive would be far more difficult. That required planning and preparation and access to a facility that met certain requirements. She'd need to be restrained, but she'd also need to be fed, provided with water, and allowed the use of a toilet. Unless she was held far out in the country, or enclosed in a soundproof space, she'd need to be prevented from calling for help. She might have to be gagged or have her mouth taped shut.

Could a single kidnapper manage to capture, control, and restrain her?

Possibly. If that person was strong enough and had the necessary facility and equipment ready.

But what did I know? I'd never held anyone hostage.

Feeling a little thrill of pleasure that Iz's attempt at investigating had been thwarted by Big Chill, and a big sinking feeling because she might somehow triumph over me anyway, I headed for Mrs. B's condo.

The sliding glass door was open a few inches, so I heard her talking as I approached. It was a one-sided conversation, and I deduced she was on the phone. From her tone, I had no trouble making the assumption that she was losing patience at a rapid rate.

"It won't matter if an attorney is the best or the worst," she said. "It won't matter if he or she has years of experience or less than a month. If a client refuses to talk, there's very little to work with besides the evidence police collect."

Cheese Puff stuck his head out and gazed up at me with an expression that seemed to be asking who I was and why I'd come. I slid the door open far enough to slip through just as Mrs. B concluded the conversation.

"I'm not trying to discourage you from helping in any way you can. I'm simply pointing out the largest obstacle in the path." Mrs. B waggled the fingers of her free hand in my direction. "If you find a way to convince him to divulge information that could help with his defense, let me know and I'll help you find representation."

"Brenda?" I scooped up Cheese Puff. "Wanting you to pry Angus Drummond out of retirement to help Aston."

Mrs. B replaced the phone in its cradle and rubbed her eyelids with her fingertips, taking care not to smudge her mascara. "The police allowed her to see him. I imagine they were hoping she could talk some sense into him."

(For the record, Brenda wouldn't be my first choice to head up a talking-sense department. I'd nominate Gertrude or Ardie. After them, I'd nominate just about everyone else on the planet with the exception of those less than three years old, those suffering from advanced dementia, and certain politicians.)

"He denies any knowledge of how the shoes got in his truck," Mrs. B told me. "But that's all he'll say. He refuses to utter a word about where he was on Saturday morning before he joined the picket line."

I already knew most of that, but in the interest of possibly learning something new, I nodded and attempted to cuddle Cheese Puff against my shoulder. He was having none of it and made himself as rigid as a concrete block. Punishment for allowing Mrs. B to take him to the vet? Punishment for failing to drop by frequently to assure him I was worried about his health? Punishment for not bringing a special treat to prove I'd missed him intensely?

You bet.

Deciding not to buy in and beg for forgiveness by offering a massage, I carried him to the sofa and plunked him on a throw pillow. He turned his back on me and lowered his front end, thus raising his bottom to further demonstrate his displeasure. I thought of a few gestures of my own but, since Mrs. B might question my commitment to him, I held back.

"I barely know your friend Aston," Mrs. B said, "but I can't imagine he would have been involved in whatever happened to Ms. Potter. Or other illegal activities of that magnitude."

"I'm not sure I'd call Aston a friend," I hedged. "At least not on the same level as you or Ardie. But I agree with the last part. Aston marches to a different drum, but he has a strong sense of morality."

"That's what Brenda said." Mrs. B plucked two glasses and a bottle of expensive rum from a kitchen cabinet. She popped a can of fruity soda, and mixed us each a drink. "That's why I don't understand why he won't say where he was or what he was doing. If it wasn't illegal or immoral, why keep it a secret?"

I pondered that as, forgetting my vow to return home quickly, I plopped into a chair beside the sofa and sipped my drink. Until the rum hit my system and dulled the pain, I hadn't realized my patches of sunburn stung. Telling myself drinking was purely medicinal, I took a healthy swig, and then continued the pondering and sipping as Mrs. B rambled about Cheese Puff's visit to the emergency clinic. "No damage beyond a possible bruise, but the vet did recommend a different brand of doggie toothpaste and I purchased a couple of tubes, one for your place and one for mine. Perhaps the visit wasn't the wisest use of my time and money, but you can never be too careful, can you? And it's only money, right?"

I nodded, thinking that if you didn't have much of the folding green to your name, you'd probably leave the "only" out of that sentence. Thinking this was a good time to show more interest in my little mutt, I asked whether he'd had any views on the political speeches.

"Slept right through them. I interpret that as meaning not one sparked his interest."

I, on the other hand, interpreted that as meaning his little belly had been stuffed so full of picnic food, he'd found it difficult to stand or move and had decided a nap was in order.

I said nothing and she went on, recapping what Deming had told me about Dario's reaction to Jake's on-air disaster, and listing the "treasures" gleaned from among Verna's hoarded possessions. I sipped and pondered Aston's silence, considering my own life and experiences and the times I'd kept quiet about events and incidents. Mostly, I decided, it was because I'd been humiliated or embarrassed, because I'd felt stupid or taken advantage of, or because I'd been mortified and felt small and weak and queasy. Could the same be true of Aston? Had the "important" thing been something he was ashamed of—so ashamed he wouldn't admit to it, not even to clear himself of kidnapping charges?

I cast my mind back over the humbling and humiliating events of my life. There were, as you can imagine, quite a flock of them. If you've been following my story, you know they include my marriage to Jake and the day I lost control of the high school horticulture class and shouldered the blame for the mud ball fight that followed. But you probably don't know about an incident from my childhood that still makes me squirm when a photo or piece of music reminds me. It began with the shame of having my chubby, stubby body stuffed into a leotard. My mother said it was for my own good because I needed to learn to be more graceful and get some exercise as well.

Next, I was dropped off to take lessons with a group of willowy aspiring ballerinas who had been dancing since about a week after birth. My rounded body and two left feet made me the butt of whispered jokes. Wanting to avoid conflict with my mother, conflict that would include several mentions of the cost of ballet lessons, I suffered in silence. Then Iz—saying silence was even more annoying than my usual chatter—questioned the reason for my zipped lips.

To my surprise, when I opened up about my feelings of shame and humiliation, she sympathized. Then, to my delight, she informed my mother she believed ballet lessons would add to her skills as a softball player and begged for the funds to purchase a leotard and enroll in my class. Horrified at what my sister could put the instructor through, my mother put a stop to my lessons.

My mind—far more agile than my body ever was—jumped from images of my younger self in ballet class to an image of Aston in a tutu. I snorted out a laugh.

Mrs. B peered over the rim of her glass. "What is it, dear?"

"Nothing. Just thinking about Jake."

Not exactly a lie. I had, after all, been thinking about him a few minutes ago.

She narrowed her eyes, but then went on, telling me she'd brought Verna out to survey the contents of her car and found her friend had no memory of any of the things that once were hers. In fact, she'd assessed the whole load as "nothing but junk no one would want for any reason."

I made an effort to listen, but my mind drifted to the image of Aston in a tutu. Could he have been doing something as out-of-character as taking ballet lessons on Saturday morning?

I sipped my drink in order to smother another snort of laughter.

Probably Aston wasn't taking ballet. But perhaps he'd signed up for ballroom dance lessons. Or swing.

But why?

Was he trying to impress Brenda? Or impress another woman?

I tried to imagine Aston in courtship mode, bathed and shaved and armed with candy, flowers, and a certificate of graduation from a dance academy.

My mind, as they say, boggled. I snorted a laugh I couldn't smother.

Chapter 29

"If you don't intend to listen, dear," Mrs. B said in a voice as tart as a sugarless rhubarb and lemon peel pie, "then I see no point in pretending we're engaging in conversation."

I bowed my head. "Sorry."

"Are you?" Her expression matched her tone. "You appear distracted. Is something wrong? Something you can tell me about?"

Since I could pretty much tell Mrs. B everything—with the exception of explicit details of bedroom-based activities—I unloaded what I knew about the kidnapping and Aston. I even confessed to fearing my sister would solve the case.

Mrs. B, of course, delivered a mild lecture about letting jealousy and sibling rivalry get the better of me. And then, after mixing us each a second and less potent drink, she got down to the business of sorting and examining what little evidence I had.

"Tell me more about that note. Are you certain the request was for only $10,000?"

"Positive. I thought it was weird, so I counted the zeros twice to be sure."

Mrs. B sipped and tapped her fingers on the arm of her chair. "I'd almost be inclined to think the money is secondary to the demand to support for the union's financial offer."

That theory made sense. But it didn't help Aston. I slouched in my chair and offered other possibilities. "What if money isn't important to the person who wrote the note? Or what if that person doesn't have a concept of what Marybeth Potter is worth and could pay for her freedom? Or what if that person doesn't have a concept of money in general? What if the kidnapper thinks the penalty might be lighter because the demand is for such a small amount?"

"All good points, dear. Any of those reasons could be valid." She sighed and sipped. "Why do you suppose Seleena Potter didn't call the police the minute she saw the note? Is she not worried about her mother?"

"From what I've gathered, she's more worried about herself and a future with a father who isn't motivated by money. But my feeling about the note is that she brought it to Doug to get his attention, make him notice her. Something he's been trying not to do for more than a year."

I filled her in on what Doug told me about Seleena as a student and how she'd been stalking him since she graduated.

Mrs. B made a tutting sound. "I guess I'm behind the times. I wouldn't have thought a high school girl would show so much interest in a teacher."

"It happens. Doug's a handsome guy who doesn't appear much older than a lot of the seniors. That's why we have training in the appropriate responses and what we should report and when and to whom if we suspect someone is crossing the line."

I explained the steps Doug took to alert the administration and have Seleena moved to another classroom. "But she didn't get the hint and she's still stuck on him."

"Sad. I'm sure there are plenty of young men who would be interested in her."

I wasn't so sure. Allison had insisted even boys found her annoying.

As if he heard me thinking that last word and assumed I was requesting a demonstration of how to be annoying, Cheese Puff leaped from his cushion and into my lap. There he circled, dug at the bare skin where my shorts ended, and nudged my arms.

"Isn't that sweet? He wants some affection, dear."

Mrs. B's tone implied that I'd better offer said affection if I ever wanted to imbibe in her condo again. I set my drink aside and rubbed Cheese Puff's knobby little head. He flopped on his back, showing his belly. I obliged with more rubbing. Apparently what I offered wasn't enough, because he pawed at my hands.

"I believe he feels you've fallen significantly behind in the attention-delivery department," Mrs. B observed.

I took a long pull on my drink in order to contain a spate of comments. Mrs. B set such a high standard for spoiling, pampering, and doting that I'd fallen short since the first moment Cheese Puff met her. I suspected only her love for me—and perhaps because Dario's views about entitled pooches were similar to Dave's—kept her from suggesting he move in on a permanent basis.

Would life with her be more to his liking?

In many ways, it definitely would. But much as Cheese Puff loved to be treated like royalty, it seemed he also loved to appear put upon and taken for granted. He enjoyed being a prince. And he enjoyed being a pest. If the chips were down and he had to pick one role, I had a sneaking suspicion he'd go with the second. Overall, it allowed for a greater range of acting, and for action and reaction.

But I didn't say any of that.

Instead I swallowed, cleared my throat, pasted on a penitent expression I didn't feel, stood, and tossed him—gently, of course—across my shoulder. "I'll do my best to make up for my failings when we get home. Thanks for the drink."

Mrs. B shot me a skeptical look, but didn't say a word.

I treasured the silence while I took Cheese Puff for a quick visit to the bark mulch in the rose garden. I treasured it right up until I encountered Allison.

She was waiting with a demand when I came through the door. "I need your car tomorrow."

"Need?" I plopped Cheese Puff on his favorite chair. He raised his upper lip at Allison, revealing his bling, then burrowed into the crevice between the cushion and the side of the chair. "Need?"

She started to pout, caught herself, and smiled. "I want to borrow your car. I have to— I want to go to the mall. I want to shop for shoes. I need new ones for when school starts."

In my opinion, Allison had enough shoes now to allow her to slip on a fresh pair every day for at least a month. But, since I also was in possession of a few more pairs than necessary, I got it. Sort of. "I thought you and some friends went to the mall Saturday morning for the three-hour sale."

"I did. But all I had time to do was the lower level."

"Why?"

"Because I saw Mr. Marsden. And after that all I felt like doing was coming home and taking a shower. Doesn't he have any clothes that don't look like they were made out of something he shot and dragged behind a truck? Or something he found in the trash behind a thrift store?"

I didn't have enough knowledge of the extent of Aston's wardrobe to provide an accurate answer. Nor did I want to do the research. But . . . Wait! "You saw Aston Marsden at the mall?"

"That's what I said." Allison's lips twitched toward another pout.

"Saturday morning?"

"Weren't you listening?" She crossed her arms. "That's also what I said."

If Aston was at the mall, he couldn't have kidnapped Marybeth Potter. Or could he? That would depend on the timing. "I was listening, but I got hung up on processing. When did you see him?"

"I told you, Saturday morning."

"What time?"

"I don't know." She stomped a foot. "I was busy."

"Right. Okay. Well, what was he doing when you saw him?"

"Duh. What does everyone do at the mall?"

"Meet their friends," I said in a snarky tone much like hers. "Hang around in the food court sharing a basket of fries. Try on sunglasses and shoes and clothes. Laugh behind their backs at anyone older than 40."

Allison rolled her eyes but didn't deny doing even one of those things. "He was going in a men's store. He was shopping. He had bags and a shoebox and stuff."

My mind boggled to the max. Sure, I knew Aston shopped. He couldn't shoot or net or dig up *all* his food. And, hard as he tried to be true to life in the past, I doubted he grew cotton or flax of whatever it took to make his shirts, socks, and underwear. But if you'd asked me an hour ago, I would have said he did his shopping at a store specializing in clothing for outdoorsmen. I would have bet the last malted milk ball in my stash that he'd never been inside the mall.

I interrogated Allison further. After all, if Aston decided to level with law enforcement and prove his innocence, she might be called as a witness. "You're sure it was him?"

Allison groaned. "Of course I'm sure. I don't need glasses like you do. I'm not old."

Ouch!

"Silly me. I forgot about that pesky age thing." I turned to hide a smug grin and headed up the stairs. "Since my aging brain is so addled, I'll probably forget you want to borrow my car tomorrow and take off with it before you're out of bed."

"Wait," Allison cried. "That's not fair. You won't really forget. You'll just pretend. And I need shoes. Mine are all gross. I can't go back to school in gross shoes."

I didn't respond and her voice faded as I reached the master bedroom and closed the door behind me. Let Dave deal with her when he woke up. Which, from the way he was sprawled and snoring, would be hours from now. Many hours.

For a few seconds I pondered shaking him and sharing what I'd learned so he could pass it on to his buddy Detective Atwell. Then I decided the story would keep. Besides, it wouldn't come down to only Allison's testimony. Surely there were security cameras at the mall, and surely Aston's image would be on some of the recordings.

And maybe the timing didn't help Aston. Maybe being at the mall wouldn't clear him of suspicion.

But if it would, why keep silent?

The embarrassment factor was a consideration, but its weight diminished when it was stacked up against spending time in a cell.

At least it did for me.

But I was a wuss compared to Aston. And he might find a cell more comfortable than some of the tents he frequented during historical reenactments.

I brushed my teeth, washed my face, pulled on the bagged-out T-shirt that passed for sleepwear, and crawled beneath the sheet beside Dave. Except for the vibrating body parts that enabled him to produce a series of world-class snores, he was as still as if he'd been embalmed.

I rolled onto my side, folded a pillow around my head to deaden the assault on my eardrums, and within seconds realized I wouldn't get to sleep anytime soon. It had been a long, demanding, and complicated day. By rights I should be exhausted. But I wasn't. My legs twitched and my back itched and my mind skittered through details of all I'd heard and thought and guessed at.

I tried tightening my muscles and then relaxing them, starting at my toes. Then I did it again, starting with my clenched jaw. I counted sheep and I counted all the good things and wonderful people in my life. I pretended I was trapped in the center row at a debate between the candidates for county assessor, listening to them cite tax rates and property values for the past 50 years.

Nothing worked.

Even imagining myself walking through a maze of supermarket aisles, each one featuring shelves crammed with cheesy snacks of every possible variety and shape, couldn't slow my bouncing thoughts or a barrage of mental images. Mind pictures of Aston Marsden at the mall. Aston Marsden shopping. Aston Marsden carrying bags. And a shoebox.

That image gave way to one of Seleena Potter, who reportedly loved shoes, teetering on the high heels of her sandals. Seleena Potter, who had a crush on Doug Whitman, bringing the ransom note to the park to show him. Seleena Potter not seeming to realize, or pretending ignorance of the fact, that police should have seen the note immediately. And Seleena Potter demonstrating darn little anxiety about her mother's safety or fate.

I brought up a mental image of the ransom note and puzzled once again over the relatively miniscule amount of money demanded. $10,000. If I were a kidnapper and facing a stiff penalty if I got caught, I'd ask for far more. I mean, why not make the risk worth it?

But someone as naïve as Seleena Potter might not think that way. Entitled and sheltered by her mother's position and income, she might have no idea what kind of a prison sentence could be meted out for the crime. She might have no idea of the value of money in general. She might not see beyond the high-end shoes and stylish clothing the ransom would purchase.

Did she intend to make at least some of those purchases in an effort to impress Doug Whitman?

Possibly.

Would Doug notice?

No.

Doug was working overtime at *not* noticing Seleena. A wardrobe overhaul wouldn't change that.

Beside, from conversations and comments in the teachers' room where I ate lunch, I knew Doug had almost no knowledge of, nor interest in, styles and fads in women's clothing. And from what I'd seen of his wardrobe—mostly khaki slacks and shirts with simple patterns and muted colors—men's clothing wasn't a passion either. Of course, his salary could be a factor. After rent and food and car payments, I doubted he had much money left.

Money!

I'd forgotten there was more than $10,000 in cash mentioned in that note. There was whatever the pay raise for teachers would amount to. And Marybeth Potter would have to agree to vote in favor of that raise if she wanted her freedom.

I sat up in bed and clapped my hand over my mouth to muffle thoughts spilling into words and phrases complete with exclamation points. "Holy smoke. Hold the phone. Would Seleena kidnap her own mother in order to get a raise for teachers as a way to get one particular teacher to notice her?"

Chapter 30

Nah.

Seleena wouldn't kidnap her own mother.

The idea was too far-fetched.

The planning would have required attention to detail.

The execution would have been complicated.

And Seleena wasn't noted for being the brightest bulb in the chandelier.

Furthermore, Detective Atwell hadn't treated her like a suspect.

Not that his instincts were always right. In the past there had been times—starting with the days when he thought I might have murdered Henry Stoddard—when he'd been off base. But this time he might be right.

Besides, this afternoon Seleena had cried for her mother.

But, as I replayed the encounter in the park, I realized those tears had dried up fast. Darn fast.

And, come to think of it, the waterworks—at least from my perspective—seemed to be caused mostly by fears about her future, and efforts to capture Doug's attention and sympathy.

Wiggling free of the sheet, I paced a circle in the space between the bed and the dresser. My mind churned, questions and theories mixing, melding, and mashing together. If Seleena kidnapped her mother, and if she meant to release her unharmed, had she disguised herself? Where was she holding her? How did she intend to handle what could be a very complicated ransom drop and collection? Did she have an accomplice? Who? Why?

I ordered my busy brain to stop tossing out fresh questions and returned to the second on my list. Where would she stash her mother?

Seleena's world, I surmised, was fairly small. From what Doug had said, I gathered she had no interest in history or visiting foreign lands, no interest in going beyond Portland. What she did enjoy, according to Josh, was flouting her mother's power, basking in the glow of it, and presenting herself as the princess frog in the puddle. Police had searched her home and the houses her mother had listed. Her mother's car had been abandoned not far from the sandwich shop, and her purse dumped near a popular swimming hole in the rural northern part of the county. According to Allison, most of the kids at Captain Meriwether High School, whether they'd been there or not, knew about the place. So Seleena most likely would have been familiar with it. And my guess was she'd strutted her bikini-clad body there at least once. Probably while wearing a new pair of sandals.

I recalled the dilapidated houses on the road to the park. Dave said they'd been searched. And since tracking dogs had been part of the search, I felt confident Marybeth Potter wasn't in an attic or basement or outhouse.

And I also doubted Seleena—if she kidnapped her mother—would stash her in an area so far from her home and the place where she worked. She'd have a long way to go to check on her hostage. And, given the terrain and undergrowth, she'd put her shoes in jeopardy every time.

No, if Seleena kidnapped her mother, she tossed the purse out there to draw attention away from the car, away from Reckless River, and away from places closer to her home, places she was familiar with.

So, what were those places?

I paced faster as I built a list.

There were movie theaters, restaurants, and boutiques in Reckless River, and across the river in Portland. But those were public places—extremely public. No way could Seleena drag her mother through a crowd and then— What? Lock her in a closet or storage room?

The storage room idea made me think of Mrs. B raiding the unit she'd rented for Verna's hoardings, picking out items she could swap on the air. Had Seleena rented a storage unit and stashed her mother there? If so, how could I find it? There were probably hundreds—maybe thousands—within a short drive of her home. I doubted storage facility managers would provide me with lists of renters or tell me whether Seleena was one of them. And if she'd used an alias to rent a unit I'd get nowhere.

I heard Allison go to her room and paced even faster, working up a sweat despite the air conditioning.

That's when I recalled Mrs. B remarking about how hot the unit was, so hot that candles had melted to puddles of wax. Unless the unit Seleena picked was air conditioned, Marybeth Potter could expire in captivity.

She might already have expired.

It was a long shot, but I made a mental note to fire up my laptop and check for cooled units. Then I went back to my original idea—a closet or storage room. Every home had closets. So did hotel rooms. But the homes Seleena had access to—her own and possibly the ones her mother had listed—had been searched. And stashing a hostage in a hotel room was a recipe for getting caught.

So, storage rooms? Almost every business had a storage room. But getting to a room while dragging or prodding a hostage would be risky. Especially on a Saturday morning. Unless it was possible to get to the storage room without going through the business, through a public space. Unless there was, say, a delivery entrance.

I paced a few more circles, wiped my forehead on a sleeve, and remembered Seleena worked at a shoe store in a strip mall. Before I'd vowed to take another route to avoid a potential glimpse of the snake at the comics shop, I'd driven by it and remembered thinking the mall had an air of abandonment verging on decay. Only five of the eight storefronts were occupied: the shoe store, the comics shop, a place trading coins and medals, another stuffed with antiques and collectibles that reminded me of items Verna had hoarded, and a space rented by a number of groups for meetings. The other three storefronts were dark. Large signs in their windows bore the name of a rental agent and those signs were curling and faded. The parking lot was cracked and pitted and the once-white lines indicating spaces were pale gray. A scraggly hedge along one side was studded with aluminum cans, plastic bags, and torn food wrappers. The only cars in the lot had been at the far end, nosed up to signs indicating the area was reserved for employees.

Could Seleena have gotten access to a vacant storefront or storage room in the mall? Were there rear entrances? Were they screened by a wall or foliage so she could drag her mother inside without being seen?

Since I'd only driven by the front of the building, I couldn't answer those questions.

However, by hopping in the car and taking a short spin, I could find out.

In a moment I was yanking on jeans and a loose cotton blouse, sliding my feet into aged running shoes, and sneaking glances at Dave. He was still snoring, fingers and toes twitching slightly. I hesitated in the doorway, recalling I'd sort of promised him I wouldn't take off on any USUIE missions.

But this wasn't actually a mission.

It was simply reconnaissance.

Yeah. Reconnaissance.

That was my story.

And I'd stick to it.

I tiptoed downstairs, dug a flashlight from the junk drawer in the kitchen, snatched my purse from the counter, and headed for the door. Halfway along the hallway I stopped, checked that I had my cellphone, and wondered if I should take a weapon of some kind. My choices were limited. I didn't own a gun and could easily name a dozen people—myself included—who thought that was a wise decision. The last time I opened Dave's jackknife I broke two fingernails. And carrying a kitchen knife without using something to cover the blade was fraught with peril—for me and my clothing.

That last word made me think of my sister and her cargo pants with the bulging pockets. She wouldn't have to think about weapons to take along on a mission. She'd have plenty already buttoned inside the compartments sewn in the fabric covering her thighs. I knew she carried at least one canister of self-protection spray, a whistle shrill enough to rupture eardrums, and a folding knife. I suspected she also stocked an assortment of other items ranging from brass knuckles to throwing stars to things I didn't want to think about.

My sister unarmed was scary enough.

My sister armed with a gun was beyond the valley of bloodcurdling.

I returned to the kitchen and surveyed the possibilities—a rolling pin, heavy frying pan, and a barbecue fork. I also considered half a bag of pork rinds I discovered wedged behind the frying pans in a cabinet next to the stove. I'm not a fan of rinds even when they're fresh, and this bag bore an expiration date back in March. I wondered if aging would qualify them as chemical weapons. I imagined throwing them at an attacker and decided, given the puffy factor, they wouldn't travel more than a few inches. I'd be better off sprinkling them in a protective circle and crushing them to release maximum odor.

"Ugh."

I was more likely to choke myself than I was to drive off an attacker.

So, forget weapons.

I mean, how likely was it I'd need protection on a simple reconnaissance mission?

I wouldn't be gone more than half an hour.

I might not even get out of the car.

I headed for the door a second time, then scooted to the kitchen again, dug an envelope from the recycling container under the sink, and wrote a note for Dave. Smug satisfaction settled over me as I did. He was forever complaining that I went off without a care in the world or the least bit of notice. He claimed that's how I always ended up in big trouble. Well, this would show him.

With an exclamation point and a heart, I finished and gave some thought to where I might leave it so he was likely to spot it. I decided to center it in the hallway at the base of the staircase. If he woke up and looked for me, he couldn't miss it when he came downstairs.

I shouldered my purse, marched to the door, and opened it to balmy twilight. I was about to close it behind me when Cheese Puff brushed past.

"Stop," I ordered in an authoritative whisper.

Without so much as a backward glance, he trotted along the walk toward the parking lot.

"Come back," I called softly.

He didn't return.

I closed the door behind me and followed, trying other commands. "Sit. Stay. Wait."

He kept moving.

I went for bribery. "Want some fresh kibble? A dog cookie? A chew stick?"

He didn't falter.

I upped the ante. "How about a piece of cheese? Some salami? A spoonful of butterscotch pudding?"

That last caused a split second of hesitation, but then he put on a final burst, darted to the canopy-covered parking area, ran a circle around my car, and came to a halt by the driver's door.

Have I mentioned that all the training and threats in the world had no effect when he was in one of his stubborn and determined moods?

If I was intent on my reconnaissance mission, it was apparent it would not be a solo mission.

I gave up, gave in, and unlocked the car. "I suppose you want to ride shotgun," I taunted.

He lifted his upper lip and his gold-capped tooth flashed in the security lighting. Again, I rued the day Mrs. B sprang for that bit of dental work after he'd chipped the tooth carrying a roulette ball on a mad chase around the casino where he'd slipped his leash and run amok. His behavior, always erratic, entitled, and ego-centric, now often crossed the line into objectionable, obnoxious, and ornery.

(For the record, since Cheese Puff weighs a mere 10 pounds, I was perfectly capable of picking him up and tossing him back inside the condo. I'd done just that several times in the past. But I'd done it during daylight hours when Dave was awake and neighbors wouldn't feel obligated to complain as much. You see, Cheese Puff frequently demonstrates his disgust for my discipline by pawing, barking, and howling. Even as tired as he was, Dave would hear. I doubted he'd make good on threats to tape Cheese Puff's mouth closed or tie mittens to his feet, but he might shut him in a closet or dump him in the clothes hamper.)

As I opened the car door I embarked on another exercise in futility. "Here are the rules for when we get to the strip mall. No barking. No wiggling out of your harness. No running off. No eating things you find lying around. And no whining to go home before I'm ready to leave. Got it?"

He raised his lip once more, but jumped in and held still while I buckled him in the spare harness I kept in the car and snapped on a short nylon leash. "No retractable leash tonight. You're going to stay close and obey."

He gave me the wide-eyed innocent expression that implied he would never disobey or wander more than a few inches from my side.

Never mind that he just had.

Chapter 31

Refraining from pointing out his track record of disobedience, I fired up the engine, a process that took four tries and a few choice words. My rolling wreck needed a trip to the repair shop. Suspecting that trip would drain my bank account to within a few hundred dollars of the bottom, I was procrastinating.

But I had no time to think about that now, so I continued with the head-in-the-sand approach to the issue. When the car wouldn't start at all, or when the wheels fell off, or when smoke billowed from beneath the hood, I'd leap into action.

In the meantime, with my fingers crossed on the wheel, I backed out of my space and eased across the speed bumps on the way to the street. No sense in shaking anything loose. Or looser.

Cheese Puff stood on the edge of the seat and planted his front feet on the dashboard. It was a stretch because I'd recently pushed the passenger seat as far back as it would go to make room for a giant package of toilet paper from the bargain store. He turned to me and whimpered.

"Not stopping to adjust it," I said. "Suck it up."

He clawed at the dashboard.

"If you're trying to give it the distressed look, forget it. The interior of this thing passed distressed years ago."

He yipped, clawed again, lost his balance, and tumbled into the footwell.

Knowing he'd seek revenge, I bit back a laugh as he clambered onto the seat once more. And I stifled anything on the I-told-you-so spectrum while he turned his back on me, planted his front feet on the armrest, and peered out the passenger window.

In a few minutes we approached the strip mall. Bits of broken glass glittered as my headlights swept across the parking lot. I rolled through the first of two entrances and surveyed the access to the rear from there. Broken pallets and bottles and the hedge—long allowed to grow wild—made me cross that choice off my list and cruise to the side with spaces marked for employees. Beyond them, pavement continued around the side of the building and I followed, clicking on my high beams as I did.

Not a single bulb illuminated this end of the building and at the back I spotted only two along the roofline. They didn't offer enough illumination for me to see if there once had been others but they'd burned out. The bulbs offered barely enough light for me to make out a narrow lane edged with what appeared to be stacks of cardboard, a broken table, and a large trash container. Beyond those, bordered by a drift of litter, was what an optimist might call green space and a pessimist would call a wasteland.

If Seleena Potter was keeping her mother here, the odds of her being spotted if she came and went at night were slim.

Unless there was a security service.

Given the lack of landscaping and upkeep, it appeared the owner either had little interest in the property, or little money to spruce it up. The coin and medal shop, I'd noted, had metal grids on the windows and door. Maybe this was an each-renter-for-himself situation. Perhaps the store owners had considered their inventory, considered the preferences of burglars and junkies, computed the risk, and acted accordingly. I mean, an antique teapot may be worth something to a collector, but if you didn't have that collector lined up before you stole the pot, you'd have to hang onto it while increasing your risk.

With a series of back and forth moves, I turned the car, angling it so the headlights revealed the rear of the building. My plan was to study the details, but there weren't many to study. No windows. And only two doors. One, at the end closest to the employee spaces, was the size of the door to my condo. The other, in the middle of the long wall, was a silvery metal overhead door, a door for deliveries. Given the state of the lane on the far side along the hedge, and the state of the mall in general, I doubted the delivery entrance got much use—at least not from those with large trucks.

I didn't see a keypad near that door and assumed it had to be unlocked from the inside. Seleena wasn't an intellectual giant, but I doubted she'd go in through the smaller door and then unlock and raise the larger one to bring her mother inside. First, that meant more time and opportunity for someone to see them. The risk was small, but it was possible someone could pull in to turn around, or toss garbage, or make a drug deal. Second, if she was acting alone, she'd have to shift her concentration from her mother for a few minutes to raise and lower the door. And third, I couldn't see Seleena taking additional steps if she could get her mother inside through the small door.

Granted, I didn't know her well, but she didn't strike me as an extra-effort kind of person. Unless that effort was expended on hair, nails, makeup, or wardrobe.

I'd made a mental catalog of the shops in this mall while driving by, but I'd never been inside any of them. And, since I couldn't see through the rear wall, I was left guessing about the layout. Was there a back door in each store leading to a common area with restrooms and perhaps a small kitchen? Were there individual storerooms for each space?

There were a couple of ways to find the answers.

One was to drive back around front and peer through store windows hoping an owner had left a rear door open and a nightlight on in the back room. As they say, hope springs eternal. Generally, however, my hope sprang only high enough to fall flat.

A second way was to drop in during business hours and ask a few questions. Not drop in on the owner of the comics store, because that might entail getting far closer to a snake than I prefer. And not the shoe store, because I wanted to avoid Seleena. That left two store owners to question, and possibly someone from a group using the fifth space. But I couldn't visit until the stores opened. And that wouldn't be until tomorrow morning.

Getting my hands on a blueprint or something similar would also involve waiting. And—I'm pretty sure I've mentioned this in the past—I hate waiting.

Cheese Puff pawed at the passenger door handle.

"You're right," I told him. "We could saunter over and see if, by some chance, one of those doors was open."

He pawed the window as if to ask what I was waiting for.

"Daylight," I told him. "This is a dark and creepy place. And you're not much in the way of protection."

He lifted his lip.

"Attitude isn't everything. You might be able to scare off a small cat or a naïve raccoon. But you'd be no match for a mugger."

He whined in protest and lifted the lip higher.

"Forget it. We're going home. It's the safe thing to do. And it's the smart thing to do."

(For the record, I can almost hear you counting up the number of times I hadn't done the safe and/or smart thing. Further for the record, I realize it's a high number. If you're seriously intent on counting every instance, it might help to get a calculator.)

While Cheese Puff snorted in annoyance, I shifted to reverse and jockeyed the car about so I could exit the way I'd come. But as my headlight beams strafed the wall, I had second thoughts. What if I pulled up beside the smaller door and hopped out for just a moment, and rattled the doorknob to see if the door was unlocked?

Even from here I could tell the knob was rusty and tilted downward. Maybe the catch was loose or the lock was faulty. I could determine that in a few seconds. And I wouldn't be more than a few feet from the car and safety.

As if to second my proposal, Cheese Puff yipped.

"Okay. But you stay here."

He pawed the seat and raised his lip.

"I mean it."

Like that ever worked with him. Or with any of the more challenging high school students I encountered.

I eased the car as close to the wall as I could. Given that I was a terrible judge of distance, I was probably no closer than two feet. Or so. Even if I'd had a ruler with me, I wasn't about to spend time measuring.

For extra insurance, I kept the headlights on the high-beam setting. Then I unbuckled my seatbelt, gripped the flashlight, and slid out.

In two seconds I was at the corner of the building. Hands braced against the concrete-block wall, I peered around the corner.

No one in sight.

Two more seconds and I was back at the door and jiggling the knob.

Just as I thought, it was old and loose.

I gripped it. With a bit of a twist and a push it might—

A hand clamped onto my shoulder.

Chapter 32

I squealed.
Cheese Puff growled.
Someone cursed.
The hand released me.

I spun about, careened off a fender, raised the flashlight to deliver a blow, spun some more, and came face to face with my sister.

"What are you doing here?" I shrieked.

Iz shook her right leg and cursed again. "Right now I'm trying to get your dog to let go of my pants."

Cheese Puff hung on, his teeth in the fabric of her cargo pants, his front legs wrapped around her ankle.

"Did you follow me?" I raged.

"Why would I follow you?"

"Because you didn't have any ideas of your own? Because you couldn't find a clue if someone painted it red and put a flag on it?"

"That's not true and you know it."

"It *is* true and *you* know it."

Iz swung her right leg back and bent her knee so Cheese Puff's rear legs dangled. "What I know is your dog will be airborne in five seconds if he doesn't let go."

I ordered Cheese Puff to release her.

He didn't.

I bent to pry him loose, but Iz hopped to the side and whipped her leg around.

Halfway through the arc, Cheese Puff let go.

He turned two aerial somersaults and tumbled into my arms with a grunt. The leash, trailing behind him, draped itself around my neck.

Unbalanced, and with a grunt of her own, Iz fell to the pitted asphalt with a thud severe enough to register on the nearest earthquake monitor.

(For the record, I have no idea how far it is to the nearest monitor. But since at least two volcanic peaks are clearly visible from downtown Reckless River, and since one erupted in a major way in 1980, I'm guessing there's a monitor within walking distance. Provided, of course, that I wore the correct shoes for the hike, set a rapid pace, and didn't make too many detours for drinks and snacks.)

"He did that on purpose," Iz howled.

Cheese Puff smirked.

"Of course he did. What did you expect?"

Iz shot me a scowl any substitute teacher would be happy to add to her repertoire, and mumbled a retort I couldn't make out. Then, with another liberal dose of cursing, she heaved herself upright and dusted grit from her rear. "Did you get the door open?"

"No. If you recall, I was interrupted."

"Probably couldn't have managed anyway. I've seen baked potatoes with more muscle than you've got."

The thought of baked potatoes—loaded with butter, sour cream, chives, and shredded sharp cheddar—made my mouth water. While I was swallowing in order to deliver a snappy comeback, Iz marched to the door, gripped the knob with both hands, pulled it toward the hinges, lifted, and pushed.

It popped open.

Iz charged inside.

I heard a series of thumps. "Light switch should be right around— Ah."

The switch clicked.

A naked bulb flashed on.

And flamed out.

The image of a long corridor lingered in my brain for a few seconds before darkness closed in.

I remembered the flashlight still in my grip. Cradling Cheese Puff in my left arm to free my right hand, I clicked on the beam.

"About time you helped," Iz growled.

I was already a snappy comeback behind and, as you know, my best retorts are wasted on Iz, so I said nothing as I played the light along the corridor. It was about eight feet wide—at least where boxes weren't stacked along the wall or leaning dollies didn't claim space. At the far end was a kitchen smaller than the one at the radio station, and about as well-equipped. A door beyond the refrigerator stood open, revealing a toilet and a sink large enough to wash one hand at a time.

Iz pointed at wooden doors spaced out along the inner wall. Each bore at least one sign, some professional and some hand-lettered. All were scuffed and scarred and speckled with bits of tape and the corners of former signs and notices. "Which one were you planning to try first?"

I didn't want to admit that I'd arrived without a plan because this had started as a reconnaissance mission, so I feigned confidence. "If she's here, she's in one of the vacant stores."

"You think?"

I aimed the beam at her eyes.

I mean, why not? Just because I didn't have a handy retort didn't mean I couldn't seek payback in other ways.

She grabbed for the flashlight. "Give me that."

I jerked away. "No. You should have brought your own."

"These are new pants," she said in a sulky voice. "The pockets are smaller. I couldn't fit it in."

I made a tutting sound. "The high price of fashion."

"Knock off the attempt at humor and tell me which stores are vacant."

I tried to visualize the front of the strip mall, tried to recall which storefronts bore signs offering space for rent. The picture I got was as fuzzy as if I'd viewed the mall without the benefit of my glasses. Except for the comics store. That was in the center. But, since there were eight stores, there were actually two in the center, and I couldn't remember if it was the one on the left or the one on the right. Further, since we were now in the rear of the building, what I'd determined as left or right from the front would be reversed.

And, to raise another issue, what if the snake didn't come and go with its owner? What if it lived in the store and had a cozy little snake bed in the back room where it curled up at night? Or coiled up? And what if it didn't curl/coil up at night? What if it slithered around at will? What if it was "employed" to deal with, say, a mouse problem?

All those questions I couldn't answer would have been enough to give me a headache if one hadn't already sprouted the minute my sister turned up. "I can't remember where the empty stores are in the order."

"Of course you can't," she snarled. "Maybe we can tell from the signs. What were they before they were vacant?"

"I don't know."

"Why not? You're the one who loves to shop."

"I don't love to shop. And even if I did, that wouldn't mean I knew the location and status and history of every store in Reckless River."

"Well you don't have to get huffy about it." Iz stomped to the first door and peered at the signs. "Get that light over here."

"Before or after I salute?"

Iz didn't answer, so I took my sweet time, taking not a single step in her direction until I positioned Cheese Puff across my left shoulder like a baby in need of burping. Then I eased her way, aiming the beam at a yellowed piece of notebook paper covered with dollar and cent signs.

Iz smacked the sign with the palm of her hand. "What the heck does this mean?"

"It means this is the store that sells and trades coins."

"You sure?"

I played the light over a deadbolt lock and noted this door, unlike the others, was no flimsy wooden model. Then I recalled the metal grids on the front and further recalled the store was the last I'd passed on my way to the rear of the building. "Positive."

"Hmmph. I guess I'll trust you." She said that in a way that implied she was doing me a huge favor or even awarding me a national honor.

She marched to the next one. A sagging sign sported a bug-eyed face with oversized glasses. I ran a mental list of the stores still open and decided this one was out of business.

"I think that one's empty."

"Let's see."

Iz put her shoulder to the door, gripped the knob and twisted. It held for the count of five and then gave up and gave in. The storeroom beyond smelled of old plastic bags and mouse droppings.

My sister sneezed, a sound not unlike the snort of a bison about to charge. She smacked the wall and a switch clicked but darkness reigned. Either the bulb was burned out or the power had been shut off to this unit. She sneezed again and stomped to the store itself, the husks of deceased beetles cracking beneath sandals almost wide enough to use as ping-pong paddles, dust swirling around her ankles in the hot and stagnant air. I followed quickly. No sense in letting the dust cloud rise farther while I lingered.

The second door was ajar and, except for two glass-fronted showcases, a listing chair, and a fly-spotted mirror, the room was empty, the dust on the floor unmarked by footprints. Unless you counted those left by mice.

I shivered despite the heat. Definitely a mouse problem here. But did that mean the snake would be on the job in the comics shop? On the job and on the loose.

"Next," Iz ordered.

I put the snake worries aside and we retreated to the corridor and the third door.

It was cleaner than the others and sported a lock a foot above the knob and two signs. The first featured a horse and carriage, the name Valerie, and a phone number. The second indicated that others who ran shops in the mall should please use the front door. "I think this is the place that sells antiques."

"Fancy name for junk."

There was, depending on the items, trends, scarcity, and demand, often some truth to that statement. But I said nothing. Agreeing about something trivial, like the date or time or weather, could lead to expectations on her part that I'd agree to non-trivial things in a future round of conversation. Or it could lead to her saying I was wishy-washy and had no opinions of my own.

In other words, this was a game I couldn't win. So I wouldn't play.

Iz grunted and moved to the next door. According to my calculations it was door number four and one of the two in the middle. I squinted at the small sign hoping for a clue, but it bore only information about hours of business. It was an old sign, torn partway through the middle, smudged with fingerprints, and held up by several generations of what had once been clear tape, but was now cracked and yellowed. A pale area with several screw holes indicated the door had once had a deadbolt lock. The knob, unlike the others, was shiny and new.

Iz tapped the door. "Well? Empty or not?"

"Let me check the next one before I decide."

She issued an explosive and guttural sigh that caused Cheese Puff to tremble. As much as he reveled in demonstrating his distaste for my sister, he also feared her.

I soothed him with a whispered promise of a special treat when we got home, and shuffled to the next door. It displayed a similar sign, but this was in even worse condition. Several of the opening and closing hours had been altered with both black and blue ink, narrowing the times the shop was open. Should I assume the many changes meant this place was in business? Or should I assume the hours of operation had eventually been whittled down to none at all and this place was closed.

I checked out the knob. It was as old and wobbly as the others, but above it was a fairly new lock. That could be a security measure. Or it could mean the owner didn't want anyone strolling in because there was a snake on the loose. I played the beam along the crack where the door met the jamb and saw the lock wasn't engaged. What was the significance of that?

"Well?" Iz joggled my arm, sending the flashlight beam into a series of loops. "This isn't a lady-or-the-tiger deal. We won't get mauled. Pick one."

I shuffled back to door number four, aiming the beam at that new knob, wondering if that indicated the store was in use, or if it meant the landlord had replaced broken hardware. Given the overall condition of the place, I wouldn't bet money on that. "Just let me take another look at—"

"Forget it. We haven't got all night."

Metal scraped on metal.

"Decision made," Iz said.

Hinges squealed on door number five. "Maybe this switch works."

I heard her hand smack the wall.

I heard a click.

Light spilled into the corridor.

And something slithered along with it.

Chapter 33

Iz let out a howl that would make an alpha wolf demand a new and improved set of vocal cords.

"Snake!"

She careened across the corridor, and slammed into the overhead door.

Like a thick ribbon, the snake slowly unfurled behind her.

I froze.

Iz, who could have run in either direction along the corridor, clawed at the overhead door and remained directly in the snake's path.

Cheese Puff wiggled and pawed at my shoulder.

"No," I whispered as I slid my right foot alongside my left, executing a small backward step. "You're not getting down."

He wiggled harder, snarling at the snake.

It had paused halfway across the corridor, its head raised, its forked tongue darting in and out. Its body was as thick as my arm and it appeared there was plenty yet to emerge from the comics shop. If I hadn't been so close to wetting myself I might have admired its butterscotch markings.

Cheese Puff yipped.

"No. You're not going after the snake. If he's hungry, you could be a snack in seconds."

"Help me," Iz bellowed over the rhythmic rippling of the metal slats she pressed against. "My feet won't function. Stop talking to your stupid dog. Do something."

"Like what?"

"I don't know. I don't care. Something. Anything."

Talk about having options.

I played my flashlight beam on the wall beside the overhead door, lighting up a gray metal box with two buttons, one red and one green. "Push the green button. Open the door. If you can't walk, fall and roll."

She pushed.

Nothing happened.

She hammered at the button.

Nothing.

"What now, genius?"

I backed up two more steps, studying the snake. It continued to taste the air, its head swaying back and forth. But it seemed to be losing interest in Iz and focusing more on the far end of the corridor.

I know next to nothing about snakes, so I wasn't about to hazard a guess about what it might see or hear or smell or feel. But the kitchen was down that way. A kitchen meant food. And food could mean mice.

"Well?" Iz shrieked. "What now?"

The snake eased toward the kitchen.

I eased two steps the other way.

"When I say go for it, run back the way we came."

"I don't think I can," Iz whimpered. "My feet are stuck."

Logical replies zipped through my brain. But this was no time or place for logic. If I wanted action, this was the time to resurrect the taunts and challenges of childhood. For her own good.

"They're not stuck. You can't move because you're lazy and out of shape."

"What?" Iz roared.

"I've seen better muscular structure on pond scum."

"What?"

"Dung beetles make better nutritional choices than you do."

"What?"

"And when it comes to making friends, there are skunks—"

With a roar, Iz shoved off from the overhead door and charged at me.

With a yelp, I leaped backward.

Iz tried to adjust her trajectory, but her feet tangled and she fell against door number four.

The knob assembly, new as it appeared to be, wasn't up to the task of keeping my sister confined to the corridor.

The door burst open and Iz tumbled through, grasping at the tail of my shirt as she fell.

Two buttons popped off. The third held. Mass, momentum, and gravity took control. I pitched through the doorway with Iz.

Fortunately, she broke my fall.

Fortunately, I twisted as I fell, preventing Cheese Puff from becoming a hairy orange pancake.

And, even more fortunately, I landed facing left instead of right. I couldn't see much, but what I could see included a dirty concrete floor, the bottom shelf of a rusty metal bookcase, a gallon jug of water, and a woman with wide and angry eyes.

Chapter 34

She was gagged with what appeared to be a pair of leggings and secured to the bookcase with enough rope to supply a dozen rodeo cowboys for life.

"Marybeth Potter?" I gasped.

The woman nodded and made the kind of noises you do when you've got a gag in your mouth.

(For the record, in the interest of safety you can simulate that without using an actual gag. Just clamp your teeth, press your lips together, and try to say something. Anything will do. If you're at a loss for words, grab the paper and try to read a few headlines aloud. You'll get the drift. You may also come to the conclusion that some of the people who make headlines should wear gags every waking moment.)

"What? Who?" Iz got to her knees. Her face was red, her eyes flared, and she jabbed a finger at me. "I came through the door first. I solved the case."

Cheese Puff snarled.

Marybeth Potter wriggled and made more gag noises.

"Maybe you saw her first, but I was in this room first," Iz continued. "You were a sorry second."

"And the snake might be third unless you close the door."

Iz paled and scrambled to grasp the edge of the door. She pulled at it, slamming it against my knees.

I yowled.

Cheese Puff joined in.

"Move," Iz ordered. You're blocking it."

I drew my knees up.

Iz bashed the door against my toes.

"Move more."

I rolled on my back and raised my legs.

Iz slammed the door.

It bounced open again.

"You broke the latch."

"Did not," Iz insisted.

I sat up. "Just hold it closed while I untie Ms. Potter."

Iz leaned on it, scowling. "*You* should hold it. It's your fault I broke it. And it's your fault the snake is loose."

"It is not!"

I released Cheese Puff and tried to work the gag from Marybeth Potter's mouth, but it was too tight. "I'm Barbara Reed," I told her. "That's my dog, Cheese Puff. He won't hurt you."

Marybeth Potter's wide and darting eyes said she doubted that.

"And that's my sister Indigo Zephyr. Try to ignore her."

Her eyes seemed to rotate in their sockets as Iz explained that if I hadn't taken so much time dilly-dallying around reading signs she never would have opened the door and let the snake out.

Meanwhile I crawled behind Marybeth Potter and went to work on the knots in the leggings. There were several, all tight, all uncooperative. And there was no give left in the fabric; it had been pulled to the limit of the elastic.

I interrupted my sister's rant. "Have you got a knife in those fancy new pants?"

Marybeth Potter groaned and shook her head. I took a wild guess that she was trying to tell me the idea of Iz with a knife in her hand was terrifying.

"I agree," I told her. "I'll use the knife. And only the shortest blade. It will be slower, but you'll be free in a few minutes."

Iz patted the pockets of her cargo pants, stepping away from the door as she did.

It opened a few inches.

A hand appeared and gripped its edge.

I screamed.

Iz whirled and shoved at the door.

The person on the other side shoved back.

Chapter 35

The standoff lasted only a few seconds, long enough for me to wonder if Seleena was stronger than she appeared. Then I wondered if she had an accomplice. Then I wondered if someone with evil intent had seen us break in and followed.

And then Dave asked, "Anyone in here call for a snake wrangler?"

"I found her." Iz stepped back and allowed him to open the door. "I found what's-her-name. I get the credit. And if there's a reward, I get that too."

"You could also get charged with breaking and entering."

"No way." Iz pointed at me. "It was all her idea. I was just following along to make sure she didn't get mugged or something."

Rolling his eyes, Dave pushed past her. "Then you better hold the door closed so the snake doesn't get in and mug you."

Iz slammed the door and leaned against it. "Didn't you catch it?"

"I don't do snakes." He pulled a jackknife from his pocket and bent over Marybeth Potter. "I called someone who does."

"He'll have you free in a minute," I told her as he worked the knife blade beneath the gag in front of her ear.

"This is Dave Martin. He investigates major crimes for the sheriff's department."

"He investigates like a snail," Iz announced. "You might have been here for months if I hadn't solved this crime."

"Continue to ignore my sister," I urged.

Marybeth Potter grunted. The gag was looser, but still on. The fabric was tough stuff.

"I thought you'd sleep for hours," I told Dave.

"I would have, but I've trained my unconscious mind to respond to the sound of the squeaky step."

"Which one is the squeaky step?"

"Not telling."

Dang.

I made a mental note to check it out the next time I was home alone. Then I moved on. "You must have found my note."

"Yep. And the fact that you left it signifies that we've reached a milestone of honesty and trust in our relationship."

I beamed him a smile.

"Except you neglected to mention which strip mall you were headed for."

Shoot.

"Then how—?"

"Tracking device." He grinned and sliced through the final bit of legging. "On your car."

So much for the trust milestone.

But at least he was honest.

Chapter 36

In a Hollywood ending, Marybeth Potter would have led the charge to vote for substantial raises for teachers. But Reckless River isn't Hollywood. It's not even close. And not only in terms of geography. It's smaller, colder, and rainier. It's less glamorous and exciting. And there's a definite shortage of stars, moguls, producers, directors, agents, camera people, and soundstages. So, what happened was the rest of the board members voted in favor of the union's latest offer and, after making it clear she didn't agree, she sat out the vote. Stan Stewart quoted her as saying she felt it was in the best interests of the community to settle things and move on.

And then, that's what she did—moved on. Saying she wanted more warmth and sunshine, she relocated to Mississippi. Personally, I think the move was about more than climate. I think political leanings and charts ranking teacher pay and state financial commitment to education might have played a big role in her decision.

Before she left she wrote a hefty check to defer some of the costs of the search. But she gave Seleena exactly nothing toward her defense and sold the house out from under her. The kid is now living with her father, getting counseling, and doing what amounts to years of community service sorting and displaying footwear donations for a charity thrift store.

Aston was released from custody without having to admit he'd been at the mall at the critical time. But although the legal system let him off the hook, I didn't. I took verbal jabs until he took me aside and satisfied my curiosity about his shopping expedition. Yes, he had been buying clothing that was modern and not handmade. The reason? He'd jumped into online dating and was falling in line with the old saying about clothes making the man. I refrained from mentioning that bathing and grooming were, in my mind, also important factors and he could achieve the earthy look without the aroma.

Because no reward had been offered, Iz got exactly nothing in the way of cash. She also got darn little in the way of publicity. Stan Stewart decided the story would have more karma at its core if a substitute teacher rescued Marybeth Potter. So I got top billing.

While Iz ranted about that and took Dave to task again about their grant-writing project, I slipped away and found the tracking device on my car.

But I didn't remove it.

At least not then.

Carolyn J. Rose grew up in New York's Catskill Mountains, the setting for her Hemlock Lake mystery trilogy. She graduated from the University of Arizona with a degree and a tan, and stayed on for graduate school. Thanks to boredom and a public service announcement on late-night TV, she abandoned literary studies for two years with Volunteers in Service to America in Little Rock. From there a series of coincidences and chance encounters led her to the land of TV news and 25 years as a researcher, writer, producer, and assignment editor in Arkansas, New Mexico, Oregon, and Washington. She's now a high school substitute teacher in Vancouver, Washington. Her subbing experiences, and her sometimes rocky relationship with the dogs in her life, led her to create the canine character Cheese Puff and the Subbing isn't for Sissies series. Other than writing, her interests are reading, swimming, walking, gardening, and NOT cooking.

Catch up with her at www.deadlyduomysteries.com

Also by Carolyn J. Rose

The Catskill Mountains Mysteries
- Hemlock Lake
- Through a Yellow Wood
- The Devil's Tombstone

The Subbing isn't for Sissies series
- No Substitute for Murder
- No Substitute for Money
- No Substitute for Maturity
- No Substitute for Myth
- No Substitute for Mistakes
- No Substitute for Motives
- No Substitute for Misinformation
- No Substitute for Momentum
- No Substitute for the Munchies
- No Substitute for Mistrust

And others
- Nightfall Bay
- An Uncertain Refuge
- Sea of Regret
- A Place of Forgetting

With Michael A. Nettleton
- Death at Devil's Harbor
- Deception at Devil's Harbor
- The Hard Karma Shuffle
- The Crushed Velvet Miasma
- Drum Warrior
- Sucker Punches

www.ingramcontent.com/pod-product-compliance
Lightning Source LLC
LaVergne TN
LVHW020707110826
845149LV00012B/2141

* 9 7 8 0 9 9 9 5 3 1 0 7 5 *